RUINING THE RANCHER

MASTERSON COUNTY BOOK 3

CALLE J. BROOKES

RUINING THE RANCHER

LARGE PRINT EDITION

Copyright © 2017 by Calle J. Brookes

For information contact:

www.callejbrookes.com

Book and Cover design by C.J. BROOKES

First Edition: 2017

REED: 06052020

10 9 8 7 6 5 4 3 2 1

1

THERE WAS A MOVIE BEING MADE IN LEVI Masterson's front yard. And Levi's sweet, innocent, beautiful, wonderful, devilishly stubborn, twenty-two-year-old housekeeper was dressed in a skimpy fairy-witch costume. Parading around in front of at least three dozen people.

Distracting him from what he actually needed to be doing.

He didn't know what drove him more insane— the inconvenience of the movie crew or the woman he had wanted for months.

Levi watched as that damned film director Rowland Bowles, Hollywood's favorite hotshot, ordered everyone around in Levi's own front yard.

Including Levi's older brother Matt and sweet little sister-in-law.

Matt had been cast into the role of Clark's best friend, a struggling rancher trying to make ends meet at the property next to the more thriving one where Gretta—played by Pip—had grown up. Matt was Gretta's love interest.

Like Bowles would have ever been able to unwrap Matt and Pip long enough for another actor to take Matt's place.

They were using Pip's father's homestead as Matt's family ranch. Levi snorted at how that copied their real life. Pip was instrumental in running that ranch day to day, along with their father.

Everything was complicated and connected lately. Levi half felt he wasn't quite finding his way through.

Especially with her.

Almost from the moment he had met Pip's youngest sister, Pandora, he had known what he wanted. What was supposed to be, even. Levi was like that; when he knew what direction his life was going to take, he went after it full throttle. Until he had what he wanted. Needed.

Unfortunately, Pandora wasn't cooperating

No matter what Levi did, that girl just didn't seem to get the message that he was interested.

Levi was fast becoming the joke of their entire family.

Well, next to his brother Nate, anyway. Nate and Pip's identical twin sister, Perci, jointly held that title. The two of them fought and bickered constantly. Levi suspected it was because of the obvious and intense attraction between the two of them. They practically caught the room on fire the moment they entered. He wished he could say the same thing about him and Pan.

They could. If she would just stop being so damned stubborn.

It was too far-fetched, too crazy to even contemplate that their eldest brother, Joel, would fall for Phoebe Tyler. Shortly after, Matt went head over heels for Pip, Phoebe's younger sister. Nate and Perci seemed made for each other—and then there was Levi and Pandora.

Four brothers, four sisters. Crazy, far-fetched. Not really all that possible. But it had happened—or it would, if Pan ever caught on. And Nate stopped fighting Perci.

No wonder the entire town was talking.

It was no wonder some of his own friends had

threatened to kick his ass for taking the last Tyler sister off the market—everyone just assumed Nate and Perci were inevitable.

Well, what was a man supposed to do? They lived in Masterson County, where attractive women—women in general—were outnumbered almost three to one. Pandora was the most gorgeous woman in the entire county. Gorgeous, sweet, loyal, brave, hardworking, beautiful, gorgeous, gorgeous, beautiful, wonderful. Perfect for him.

It might have been a mistake to tell his buddies to keep their paws off her at a county dance once, but how was he to know the woman would hold a grudge for more than six weeks? All through Pip's, Perci's, and Matt's recuperation after the barn had burned and they'd all been injured, after Pip and Matt's wedding, after all of that, you would think the woman would've forgiven him by now.

She still continued to question him about why he would do such a thing. She alternated between that and ignoring him—or treating him like a slightly stupid younger brother.

Dammit, Levi was tired of her looking at him like a brother. He was also tired of that idiot director Bowles putting his hands on her.

Something had to change, and soon. Before he went totally bonkers, gave his share of his ranch to his brothers, and moved to Australia to raise crocodiles or something. Or maybe head to Antarctica. Maybe that would put enough distance between him and the woman who invaded his dreams at night.

2

Pandora Tyler knew Levi was watching her from the window. He kind of stuck out around here. Taller than many of the men crowding onto the ranch now, stronger, broader, less polished—Levi would stand out wherever he was. He might have thought that he was hidden, but he wasn't. She could have told him that.

If she wasn't getting such a kick out of upsetting him, she would have.

Levi, the biggest player in Masterson County, deserved everything he got.

She'd finally figured him out.

The entire reason he'd hired her as his house-keeper wasn't because she had worked her tail off to build a cleaning business in Masterson like she had originally thought. Taken pride in.

It wasn't that at all.

Nope; that jerk wanted her at his place where he could seduce her. Levi had planned it out, plotted all of it. Schemed from the very beginning. Gotten her right where he wanted her.

Except for *one* thing.

Tylers were not easily seduced. Every choice they made was because they believed in it. Even her older sisters, Pip and Phoebe—who had fallen for two of the nicer Masterson brothers—had done so out of choice.

If Levi thought Pan was an easy mark simply because she was a Tyler and young and living on his ranch, well, he had another thought coming. Someone called her name, and Pan spun, the gossamer dress she wore shimmering out behind her.

She had to admit she was having a blast playing a fairy in a Rowland Bowles movie. A *Rowland Bowles* movie, of all things. Six months ago, she never would've imagined it. But she, all three of her sisters, and all four of her brothers had parts. As did all five of her female cousins. She and Nikki even had major roles. Well, semimajor roles. The biggest supporting roles had gone to the twins. They played royal fairy twins who had been separated at birth to protect them. Pip was Gretta. It was perfectly suited for her painfully quiet and shy sister. Perci played the fiery new fairy queen, who was in search of her missing sister.

But it was little Parker who had surprised them all with how well he had taken to acting. He was doing so well that Rowland Bowles had modified Parker's part to be a larger piece of the entire movie. He had done the same to Pan, though she hadn't wanted him to.

While she was enjoying herself, and she thought most of her siblings were as well, acting was not something Pan ever intended to do again.

The only reason she'd agreed to do it in the first place was because of the cold, hard cash. Rowland Bowles paid very well, and with every one of her siblings in the movie, and their family homestead being used as the location, they were going to make just enough money to be able to finally pay off the massive amount of medical bills that had hovered over their heads since her mother's death almost two-and-a-half years ago. They needed that cash to fix everything.

Pan was in charge of the family finances, and she had spent those last two years sick with worry over where the money was going to come from. The scheming and the worrying and the fear were finally almost over.

And then she'd be able to get on with her life.

Pan wasn't about to let that life be tied to some man ten years older than she was and rooted in Masterson County, Wyoming.

Not that Pan *wanted* to leave her hometown. She just wanted to explore all her options first. Before considering a man like Levi. She had goals. And for the first time in two years, a way to achieve them.

Levi could derail all of that.

She'd scrimped and saved to even take a few business classes online, and if the college hadn't offered some minimum financial aid, she wouldn't have been able to afford it at all.

She'd finished those classes a few weeks ago. Now it was time to take that knowledge and apply it. Somehow.

Not that it was all that easy to use business skills scrubbing Levi Masterson's kitchen floor and folding his underwear.

That it was now her oldest sister's floor didn't really matter in the scheme of things.

Levi had hired her to do a job, and she did it to the best of her ability.

But the jerk had also hired her under false, nefarious, male circumstances. She was going to teach him a lesson about that.

As soon as she figured out how.

"Pandora, my sweet, sexy little fairy, I need you right here." The director stepped up behind her. Bowles was a touchy idiot; that was for sure. He put his hands on her hips and moved her into position for the next shot.

Good thing Pan was flexible. But it was close. The guy expected too much; she wasn't a contortionist.

Nor was there anything sexual in his hands on her hips. The instant she'd signed the contract with his company—and her siblings had done the same—he turned into a ruthless professional.

The man was good at what he did, and that was entertaining the masses.

Pan would never forget this experience.

She said her lines and knew she nailed it when Rowland crowed his pleasure. Then it was Parker's turn and her smallest brother, dressed in a fairy archer's costume, ran across the scene with panic in his movements. Just like he should have. Just like they'd rehearsed.

"They are coming! You must run!" he said, frantically. "You must go. Take this." He thrust the prop into her hand then turned. The camera focused on her then, and Parker hurried out of the way, another camera capturing his movements.

He was enjoying himself, and wasn't quite old enough to feel all the nerves that Pan was feeling. She was enjoying this gig, but it wasn't easy.

The money was good. And that mattered.

And that money was going to buy her family's freedom. Get her brothers a better chance at a future than she and her three sisters had had.

That was Pan's ultimate goal. To see to it that her little brothers were free to achieve their dreams.

The way she, Perci, Phoebe, and Pip hadn't been able to.

3

LEVI WAITED UNTIL FILMING WAS DONE AND headed toward the small bungalow that had once housed the foreman of the ranch before the Masterson brothers had purchased it to expand their neighboring spread. Rowland Bowles was renting it for the duration of his filming in Masterson.

Levi knocked with clear purpose. He and Bowles had some business to take care of.

The door swung open.

A petite strawberry blonde stood in front of him.

It wasn't Pan.

This little redhead had green eyes behind

thick glasses. She wasn't quite as pretty as Pan, but close.

Just as fiery. He'd learned that over the last two months.

She worked as Bowles's right-hand assistant, along with a real prick, Andrew, but Levi didn't think she liked her boss much. She certainly spoke to him with a snip in her tone on a frequent basis.

He wondered why she was even with Bowles. But she was extremely smart—no doubt, she had her reasons.

She and Pan and the Tyler sisters were becoming good friends. No wonder, with the way they were always together now.

"Levi, what can I help you with today?"

"I need to see Bowles. He around?"

"He's taking a shower." There was ire in the girl's tone, and disgust. "He'll be out in a minute."

"I haven't gotten in...yet. Jenny, don't you have things to do?" The other man came up behind her, dressed only in a towel. He smirked at his assistant. "Mousy type things?"

"Yes, Mr. Bowles, right away, Mr. Bowles. I live to serve, Mr. Bowles..." She left the front porch, muttering as she went.

"Hard to find good help these days," Bowles said, watching her go. "And I don't think Jenny likes me much anymore. She hasn't since the barn burned."

"Could it be that you're walking around practically naked in front of her?" He looked at Bowles. The guy was a few years older than Levi, and looked like the sleek Hollywood type. Pan had certainly mentioned how attractive she found him. Repeatedly. "Aren't you worried about her complaining?"

"Of course, I am. But I'm not ever going to touch her that way. I just want her to go back to Hollywood and leave me be." Bowles growled out his frustration. "Before I do something completely stupid."

"Excuse me?"

"You have to know what I mean. I've seen you with Pandora. There she is, right in front of you. And you want to touch. You'd change your whole world for her. In an instant, just to make her smile, make her look at you like she's proud of you. Just for that moment. And she just doesn't see. But the difference between you and I, Mr. Masterson, is that I know *I* am not the kind of a man a woman like Jenny needs in her life. She belongs in a place like this, not my world."

"Didn't you bring her with you from your world?" Poor schmuck. He looked pitiful. All over that girl.

But Bowles was right. Levi felt the exact same way.

"That's beside the point. Jenny needs to leave before she ruins everything. Why are you here?"

To break the guy's fingers for touching Pan today. But after Bowles's confession, how could he do that?

He understood the guy after all.

It sucked to be in love with a woman who just refused to see it.

He made some lame excuse to Bowles about needing the back barn in two days and hurried away.

Levi needed to find Pan. Just like always. He spent more time hunting his housekeeper than he did running the biggest spread in Masterson County. What did that say about his mental state again?

He was losing it, and he knew it.

4

SHE WASN'T STUPID. JUST BECAUSE SHE
hadn't ever slept with a man—or even kissed one
—didn't mean she was clueless when one was attracted.

And when that man was staring—again—it was
hard to miss.

Levi was interested; and that meant that he
thought he had the right to control what she did.
She had no idea where he'd gotten his archaic no-
tions. The rest of his brothers weren't that barbaric
or chauvinistic. They were good, kind, compas-
sionate, loving, and wonderful men—even Nate
who tended to give Perci fits every chance he
could.

She really liked all the Masterson brothers, Levi included.

Pan just didn't know what she wanted to do about him.

It didn't help that he was right there—everywhere—every time she turned around. Between the work she was juggling as his housekeeper, the movie and all that it required, and still trying to keep her bookkeeping business afloat, she was getting worn out.

But Pan wasn't about to complain. Of course not; Tylers never complained. Tylers just dealt.

She finished cleaning the kitchen and putting all the dishes away. They'd had everyone over from her father's house tonight.

It had been one of Perci's rare nights off.

Pan winced.

Somehow, Perci and Nate were working the same schedule again. Talk about mood killing. The two of them were getting ridiculous. Perci should just kiss him already, or something. Get it over with.

She understood her sister's hesitation.

Perci still lived with their father, and Pan didn't see that changing anytime soon. Someone had to help with the boys, especially with Perci's limited schedule. Phoebe spent her days over there, tending to her goats and the children; Pip drove her over daily. Pip spent most of her daylight hours helping their father run the ranch, along with Pete, their sixteen-year-old brother.

When Pip wasn't doing that, she was in town at Matt's vet office, helping him where she could. Or just being with him because she loved him.

Or making that damned movie. No one had expected Pip's part to be quite as large as it was. And her extremely introverted sister was wearing down. Everyone could see that. Pan was worried. And so was Matt. It was in his eyes.

He'd scooped Pip up into his arms right after dinner and carried her off to the room just off the back hall that they now shared. They would be moving out to their new home—Matt had had to remodel it first—within the month. They had managed to meld their lives together seamlessly.

As if it had been *easy* for them.

The way their mother had always promised it would be.

Just like Joel and Phoebe had somehow made things fit, easily. It was supposed to be *easy*.

But nothing about Levi Masterson was ending up easy at all. Not for her.

"Are you thinking about me?" He came up behind her after the last of his brothers left the kitchen. She fought a shiver as the scent of the mountains and Levi hit her. Yes; she was thinking about him. But Pan wasn't about to tell him that. It might do him some good to stew a while longer; she wasn't about to give into his Levi Masterson charm.

Levi stepped into her path and grinned. She resisted rolling her eyes; it wasn't fair that men like him were free to walk around without a warning sign.

She could see why so many women in Masterson County found a reason to stop by whenever Levi was home. He wasn't the tallest of the brothers—Nate towered over the rest of them—but he was still well over six feet tall, maybe six three or six four, had linebacker shoulders that he often had encased in soft-looking flannel shirts, and the man was just made for jeans and cowboy boots. Add in the face that was too perfect for a woman's sanity, and it just wasn't fair.

Sometimes when he smiled at her she turned into an idiot and forgot what it was she was thinking. Well, most times. Levi had a way of making her forget every plan she had ever made. "Of course not, I have better things to do with my time. I'm just...going over my lines for tomorrow. I think I'm supposed to seduce a mortal. Maybe that's the day after. I may get to kiss Hunter. I'm not sure yet; it all depends on what Rowland thinks."

She bit back a smile, knowing that that was sure to goad him. Levi did not like Rowland Bowles—or Hunter Louis Clark. She knew exactly why. And it wasn't because of their ridiculously pretentious names.

"Really?" Levi took the clean plates from her and lifted them into the cabinet. Pan tried to step aside, but that didn't work. Two strong arms came down on the countertop next to her, trapping her between them. "You sure you want your first kiss to be on camera?"

"What...what makes you think it will be my first kiss?" Damn those sisters of hers. One of them had definitely squealed.

But she would plot revenge against her sisters later. Right now she had an even bigger threat to worry about.

Levi smelled like he always did, that faint minty-and-wood-and-man scent that she would always associate with him. Until him, she had never really paid much attention to how a man smelled before—unless he needed an obvious shower. Not until Levi.

Sometimes when she wasn't paying attention and he got too close she would just breathe him in like a total idiot, like one of those fawning goobs from town.

And good for them. She hoped one of them finally caught him and took him off her hands quickly. With all the changes that had been going on in her life lately, Pan wasn't sure what the future was going to hold for her; she didn't like it when she didn't know the plan.

Not knowing left too much to chance, too many ways things could go so horribly wrong. Not having a plan drove her nuts.

And she had no doubt that Levi could make a woman go far, far too wrong.

"Well, am I wrong? Family rumor has it that you've been too smart to get involved with some random man. Speculation is you've never even been kissed before. So you're going to let some strange actor that you don't really know be your first?"

"Why is it any of your concern?" No, she hadn't exactly been too fond of the idea. But there was no way she was going to tell someone that she was twenty-two years old and hadn't ever been kissed.

It just hadn't happened.

After her sister Pip had been sexually assaulted at the community center parking lot when Pan was seventeen, it had left a lasting impression. Everything that had happened since that night had just made it impossible for her to get involved with a man.

At least not enough to trust him well enough for any type of physical feelings to develop. Or to let him close enough to kiss her, anyway.

Well, she was certainly close to a man now. Pan trembled. She had to admit there were definitely some physical feelings between them.

Damn Levi Masterson; he had a real way of ruining her plans.

5

Levi knew what he was doing was a big gamble. He was pushing the boundaries between them, and he knew it. She hadn't exactly asked him to kiss her.

Of course, she hadn't moved away from him either. Pan rested her hands on his chest, and he could feel them trembling. He bit back a smile, knowing he had his girl exactly where he wanted her. Finally.

Pan was attracted to him. He knew it. She was just so damned afraid.

Just like her sisters had been with his brothers. Tylers had a lot of reasons to be fearful. Matt and

Joel were helping their wives heal. Like he intended to do for Pan. If she would just let him in.

"Pan, baby girl. I really don't like the idea of some other man kissing you before I get to. What if you like him better than me? I'm...self-conscious." He deliberately grinned at her and toyed with the edge of her apron.

"It's highly likely that I will. What are you doing? Levi..."

He brushed a thumb over her lips, marveling again at how soft she was. This woman did something to him in ways he'd never be able to explain. "Pretty girl, I'm not ever going to hurt you. I want you to know that I'll never hurt you. Let me kiss you, Pandora Claire."

6

PAN KNEW WHAT SHE WAS DOING WAS CRAZY; letting him kiss her was one of the worst mistakes she could ever make. This guy was dangerous to every plan she could possibly create, and she knew it. But that didn't help. She knew the truth—she wanted *him* to kiss her.

She wanted Levi Masterson to be her first kiss. His mouth was right there. Pan struggled not to stare at it.

Levi dropped his hands to her waist. Pan squealed when he lifted her off her feet and sat her on the countertop. It put her much closer to those lips of his. Too close.

Damn him. He was just too good at all of this.

Far better than she could ever hope to be. She wished she could pause him right where he was, just long enough to run to one of her sisters and find out what it was she was supposed to do now. And then what to do next.

They were around all the rest of the time, getting all up in her business. But now that she needed them...where were they when she really needed them?

This was something she would never understand. She just wasn't any good at understanding men.

She didn't think she ever would be.

"What are you doing?" Why did she have such a stupid question? She knew exactly what he was doing. Her hand slipped over his shoulder, almost as if it had a mind of its own.

"You know exactly what I'm doing. I'm going to kiss you, baby."

Levi leaned in. Before Pan even realized it, she was leaning in toward him, too. His lips brushed hers, once. Lightly.

He pulled back slightly and looked at her out of those Masterson eyes of his. Almost as if he was questioning. When she didn't protest, he leaned in again. Brushed his lips a little bit more firmly against hers.

It tickled; she hadn't expected that. Pan gasped; Levi took advantage.

His mouth opened over hers, and for the first time in her twenty-two years, she was getting a real kiss from a man she couldn't stop thinking about.

7

LEVI DELIBERATELY KEPT THINGS AS SIMPLE AS possible. He didn't want to frighten her, and for all her sass, it would be entirely too easy to do just that. So even though he wanted to devour her—she tasted just as sweet as he had always known she would—he didn't. He kept the kiss brief and un-threatening. When he pulled away, she stared up at him. Her lips were pinker now, swollen from his, and trembling.

He forced himself to take a deep breath before he dove into her the way he wanted. He had had it bad for this woman since the moment he had first seen her—Levi wouldn't risk losing her by acting like a damned caveman the first time he truly got his hands on her.

"There, now you've had your first kiss. And, honey, when you're ready for the next one, I'll be right here waiting. You have ruined me, Pandora Claire, ruined me for any other woman. I can't think straight when you're around. I don't want to think straight when you're near. So, when you're ready, I'm going to be right here. You keep that in mind."

Turning from her at that moment and walking away was one of the hardest things he had ever done, but Levi did just that.

Pandora was far too important to him for Levi to screw everything up. And he knew it.

8

SHE COULDN'T GET HIM OUT OF HER HEAD. PAN tried as she got ready for bed in her tiny little apartment over Levi's garage. She brushed one hand against her lips like an idiot.

He'd just been so good at it. She thought. How was she supposed to know differently?

She could still feel him pressed up against her. Could smell him all around her. Damn him.

She was not going to let Levi Masterson do this to her. He was not going to change everything.

Pan snuggled in her bed and thought about him, and thought about him, and thought about him like lovesick teenage girl.

He was not going to do this to her no matter how good he was at it.

Still, as far as first kisses went—in her limited experience—kissing Levi Masterson hadn't been all that bad. In fact, it hadn't been bad at all.

No wonder she was so darned confused.

Pan flipped in the bed again, trying to ignore the fact that the sheets were the exact same color as that dork's eyes.

Mastersons were apparently really good at driving Tyler women nuts. She fought the urge to text Perci; her unmarried sister would understand, would commiserate, at least.

But Pan didn't.

She wasn't ready to share that she'd had her first kiss—and was now completely tied up in knots. Pan brushed a finger against her lips again. Let herself remember how it had felt, confusion aside. How it had felt. She fought a smile.

Levi was a really good kisser. She was glad he'd been her first.

Pan had a big day tomorrow. She had to be playing her A game for this entire movie thing to work. Too much rode on it. She couldn't let him distract her. Kissing him would definitely distract her. He already had—she was supposed to be sleeping, not wondering about Levi Masterson.

Damn him. That man could so ruin all her plans.

Pan was just going to have to not let him.

9

LEVI WATCHED THE FILMING AGAIN THE NEXT day. He wasn't about to stand by and let her kiss just any old guy. Not his girl. For all her bravado yesterday, he'd known she was nervous. She thought he didn't get it, but he did.

Levi knew she wasn't fully enjoying what she was doing. But for Pan, her family came first. She was doing this to help her family; no one else saw it, but he did.

Pan had a streak of family loyalty a mile wide. It was one of the things that he'd first noticed about her and her sisters. There wasn't anything they wouldn't do for each other. Kind of like him and his brothers. How could a guy not fall for a woman like that?

Levi was no saint, and he'd never claimed to be. He'd kissed more than his fair share of the women in Masterson County. He knew he had a reputation, but he also knew the kind of girl he'd been searching for over the last decade.

He'd taken one look at her that day they'd gone looking for Joel and Phoebe, when those damned Rutherfords had threatened his brother and the tiny woman who had become his first sister-in-law. And he'd known.

Pandora had been clutching a rifle, willing to protect the little brothers still inside their home. She had looked so young, so beautiful, and so brave...

And terrified. Something had gone straight through his gut, and he'd known that it was *his* job to take care of this woman for the rest of their lives. This was his girl, and there wasn't anything he wouldn't do for her.

And he was going to be there for her today in case she needed him.

Bowles had his actors in position. But Pandora was the focus of this one. Pandora and that damned Hunter Clark. The guy was too smooth for Levi's liking. And he'd made no bones about the fact that he found the two unattached Masterson sisters more than a little attractive.

Clark was a player, and Levi recognized the type. He was a reformed player himself, after all.

He definitely didn't like the idea of Clark kissing Pandora.

10

Hunter Clark was a professional.

His current costar and on-screen love interest most definitely was not. She was talented, but her inexperience showed.

He didn't know yet whether he wanted to pursue her or not; he'd certainly never had trouble getting a woman once he decided he was interested. And not just since becoming one of Hollywood's top male leads in the last five years.

No, if he wanted little Pan Tyler, he would have her. No matter what Bowles had to say about his actors sleeping with the neophytes that Bowles somehow always seemed to collect.

Hunter had been looking forward to the scene

with Pan for days. He wanted to have her in his arms. Just once. Before he decided.

Still, she was young, and he didn't like the idea of embarrassing her in front of the crew. He would behave himself, no matter how hard it was. Sometimes getting beneath Bowles's skin was so worth it.

He crossed the set to her. It was an outdoor shot, filmed in the early morning. She was in her human garb and not her fairy costume. So pretty. It was a good day to kiss a pretty, redheaded fairy girl. Even if it was all pretend.

It was a fall day—exactly like it was on the script—she looked beautiful, wholesome, loving, lovely. It was the red hair that first caught a man's attention.

Hers was a lighter shade, but still more red than gold. The twins and the eldest sister, Phoebe, all had darker red mixed with brown, but Pan's had enough gold to make it look like fire in the sun.

They all had those ridiculously blue eyes. Pale, flawless skin, petite bodies that were exquisitely curved. They had some cousins floating around with the same coloring, and he'd taken a look at a few of them as well. They weren't as intriguing as Pan. It was her mind that caught him. Had him wondering if he should push to get to know her better, to compete with Levi Masterson for her.

Pan had a mind like a steel trap, and five minutes of conversation with her made that very clear. She was not meant to be an actress, and Pan knew it. But she was giving one hundred percent to Bowles.

She was a businesswoman first, and this movie of Bowles's was just her way of cementing that.

Levi Masterson was a real anomaly, though. Two of Pan's sisters were married to two of Levi Masterson's brothers. Perci was just as gorgeous and intriguing, but Hunter had learned his lesson with women like Perci before. He was staying far away from her. Highly intelligent but fiery as hell. Women like her terrified him.

Pan was the one who intrigued him the most. He'd always considered himself a businessman; he knew his brand inside and out. She was just figuring her way into the business world, but he suspected that this woman would succeed. He'd always found ambition attractive. And intelligence. Far more than a pretty face, Hunter prized intelligence.

Too bad so many of the women he came across in his line of work now only saw his outward appearance. His reputation and fame. They didn't realize that he was a man with a plan, a man on a mission, a man whose very future was at stake. Hunter was a planner, as well.

The woman he was about to kiss for the first time could possibly understand exactly that. He looked toward the crowd watching the filming, his gaze landing on a particular rancher.

He had always enjoyed a challenge, after all.

Hunter smirked.

He just had to get her away from Levi Masterson first.

11

PAN COULD PRACTICALLY FEEL HIS EYES ON her. She told herself that was ridiculous—people could not really feel eyeballs.

Pan had never quite understood that expression until now. She darted a glance at Levi; he was staring at her.

Just watching, like he always did. She swallowed and squared her shoulders—it was just Levi.

Just Levi, funny.

She got through the scene, probably because she was more focused on Levi than on being nervous about kissing one of the hottest actors in Hollywood. Even when Hunter took her in his arms as Bowles directed, there was nothing. No flutter of nerves, no anticipation. Nothing like it had been with Levi. Of course, they were working at the moment. Nothing more. But she should have at least felt something, right?

It wasn't a bad kiss...she didn't think. Hunter Clark definitely didn't leave her feeling all wobbly kneed like an idiot.

Not like Levi.

What did it mean for her that one of the hottest men in the world did nothing for her, but some arrogant playboy rancher had her practically ready to forget every plan she'd ever made? None of it made any sense.

Hunter leaned down near her ear as they finally walked off the set for the day. He was a tall man, at least six foot three. Not as tall as Levi, though he was still a good ten inches taller than she was. Levi just seemed bigger all around.

She was going to have to find a way to deal with the man and she knew it.

It was better to start now than sit around and be a wimp about it.

Levi looked at her; she didn't look away, not even when Hunter leaned down and tried to talk to her again.

"You didn't do too badly today," the man said.

"Although I could sense your heart wasn't in the scene today. You have a problem with your boyfriend?"

She finally looked away from the rancher and stared at the actor. "No, he's not my boyfriend or anything like that. I'm not involved with anyone. Not really."

A part of her felt disloyal even saying that. Which was ridiculous. She wasn't involved with Levi, no matter what he and the rest of the town seemed to think.

"So the fact that Masterson over there hasn't stopped staring at you or glaring at me since Bowles called cut means nothing?"

Well, she wouldn't say that it meant nothing. Because it did mean something. She just didn't know what yet.

"It's not like that with me and Levi. He's just my boss."

"Really interesting. Very possessive boss. It's because of the family connection, I assume? Because your sisters are all involved with his brothers, he thinks he has control of you?"

Pan wasn't stupid. She knew what the man was trying to do. He was trying to alienate her from Levi. Why was he doing that? She had certainly given neither man...well, she had certainly not given *this* man reason to think she was interested.

She'd kissed Levi Masterson. She had now kissed a total of two men in her life and both of them were looking at her. Pan didn't know what to do, so she chose the most strategic option.

She retreated.

12

Hunter Clark. That little pain in the ass Pan Tyler had gotten to kiss the Hunter Louis Clark. It wasn't fair. It wasn't right at all!

Pan Tyler didn't deserve that.

Why didn't anyone else see that the girl was trash? All the Tylers were. Everyone knew that—constantly getting into trouble, constantly causing trouble. Two of her sisters had almost gotten Matt and Joel killed, after all. Didn't that matter? It wasn't right that all those Tylers were taking all the Mastersons.

Viv had had a thing for Levi Masterson since they were teenagers. But other than a few dates back in high school, he had barely looked at her.

Once he was finished sowing his oats everywhere around the county—it seemed like he had dated almost every single woman under the age of thirty in Masterson County—he was going to finally come back to her, where he belonged.

But not if that bitch Pan Tyler got her hooks into him first; she half feared the other woman already had.

Ever since that last dance at the Masterson community center, it had been clear to the entire damned town that Levi was being led around by the balls by that woman—a girl almost ten years younger than he was—who cleaned houses for a living.

She was his damned housekeeper. Surely Levi knew better than to get involved with the hired help. The mere idea of it was disgusting.

Yes, Tylers were physically well put together— the Tyler who worked as her father's foreman certainly was—but they were trash. Everyone knew that. If they weren't, she'd have sampled that Tyler herself.

Viv had grown up with two maids; well, one maid and one housekeeper, who had been paid to see to her every need. She certainly didn't consider them her equal.

People like that never were equal to people like her.

Levi Masterson was tall, good-looking, wealthy in his own right, and a damned fine catch. One of the best around this Podunk place.

She'd considered leaving Masterson County before, but her father had made it clear that if she wanted to keep the lifestyle she was now accustomed to—he was one of the wealthiest ranchers in Masterson County—that she was going to have to stay close to him. Her father had insisted she learn the business of ranching, something she absolutely despised, as well as managing his other assets. He told her before that she had to work with her mind in order to inherit what he had worked on with his hands.

Her daddy had weird ideas like that. He'd given her everything she wanted as a kid, but once she became an adult, he expected her to work for it.

Her daddy worked close with Levi. And he'd forced her as an eighteen-year-old girl to go to the Masterson place and learn, right alongside with him, as he'd done business with the older Masterson.

Everyone knew Pan's sister Perci had her

hooks in Nate Masterson really good. It was just a matter of time before that bitch took him off the market too. Just like her twin had taken Matt and the eldest sister Phoebe had taken the sheriff.

Viv hadn't wanted the doctor, the vet, or the sheriff. If she had, she would have gotten them long ago. No, she wanted Levi.

He was perfect for her needs. If she married Levi, he could take over everything her daddy was forcing her to do—not to mention he was the prettiest man she'd ever seen. Perfect and sculpted. He looked better than that damned Hunter Clark, hands down.

She'd always had what she wanted, and Levi would be no exception.

She just had to deal with Pan Tyler. The girl would come out on her feet after she lost Levi; her type always did. Hell, she'd probably capture someone exactly like Hunter Louis Clark or even the director, Rowland Bowles.

Especially in a county where women were outnumbered, that girl wouldn't stay unattached for long. Some damned cowboy would snap her up in a heartbeat.

Viv just had to detach her from her Levi. Somehow.

13

JOHN RUTHERFORD HUNKERED DOWN BEHIND the smallest barn on the Masterson place and watched everything that was happening. With all of the people coming and going from the Masterson's place, with the movie crew, plus all the hands, no one ever really looked at him. He'd been walking the back edge of the Masterson property twice a week for weeks now. Just watching. No one ever even gave him a second thought.

Of course, he had made that happen deliberately. He'd had nowhere else to go but Masterson County. He didn't have any money, didn't have any family now, either. His brother Tom had been it.

He hadn't even been allowed to go to the funeral. He was reduced to hunkering down in an old barn on the Mastersons' property that no one ever came to anyway. He bounced between it and an old cabin no one even remembered existed high up in the mountains. Like him. He had all but been forgotten.

John risked it; he had to wipe the drip from his nose before it drove him insane. He was hidden well enough. And those Mastersons were too damned sure nothing could be wrong on their place they didn't even notice him. Again.

John would probably spend the rest of his life trying not to get noticed. And it was all because of them.

A couple of the Masterson brothers were working with the bull, two hundred feet away from where he hid. John had laid there in the dark for hours.

He and that bull had tangled before. But he'd taken care of that yesterday. All it had taken was that old box of rat poison he'd found in the corner of the shed.

Bull was now as sick as the proverbial dog. John was surprised the animal wasn't dead yet. He thought one of the brothers was the vet. And it made sense. The other one had to be that damned rancher himself. All those Masterson assholes looked alike.

Just like those bitches who had caused his brother to die. He saw them running around the ranch sometimes. Especially that twin who'd married a Masterson and that one who was supposedly their housekeeper.

He'd gone to school with the Tyler twins and their slightly younger sister. He knew enough about them to recognize them when he saw them but not enough to tell the three older ones apart at a distance. Damned Tylers were the reason why his brother was dead. Those Tylers and Mastersons had ruined everything.

The very least they deserved was to lose that bull of theirs.

Well, John had already taken care of that. And as soon as those assholes were out of his way, he'd hike the seven miles between the Masterson spread and the one directly behind it—he needed to make a purchase from the one woman in town who knew exactly what he needed, and wouldn't turn him in to that damned sheriff.

14

Movie actress by day, housekeeper by night. Pan finished cleaning the floors quietly, her mind on what had happened that day. She'd kissed Hunter Louis Clark—the Hunter Louis Clark, the honest-to-goodness hottest guy in Hollywood. She had kissed him and had felt practically nothing.

In fact, she'd spent the whole kiss thinking that she wished it was *Levi* playing her love interest the way his brother was playing Pip's. Wishing it had been Levi she was kissing again.

And that was just stupid. Pip and Matt were in love, married; it made sense, the two of them being together on screen.

Pan felt like an idiot.

She scrubbed the floor a little harder than she possibly should have. She was so consumed what she was doing, what she was thinking, that she didn't hear the door open behind her until it was too late.

She looked back over her shoulder, the devil she expected to see right there. Levi often came up behind her when she was on her hands and knees. He always had a particular *look* in his eyes when he did. A look that she didn't quite understand, but one that made her extremely wary. She dropped the cloth back into the bucket and stood.

She didn't like it when he loomed over her like that. He was big, strong, beautiful—was it any wonder she felt a bit intimidated by him right at that moment?

"Levi, I saved you some leftovers." He had been up in the back pasture dealing with some sick calves, along with Matt. She had automatically saved him a plate like Pip had saved one for his brother. She'd tried to tell herself that it wasn't because she was concerned about him or anything like that.

But she had been.

Levi hadn't been able to make it back in for lunch. He hadn't taken anything with him, either.

She was just being a good housekeeper; she was paid damned fine money to take care of him.

Well, him and the rest of his family. Including her sisters. She tried to push the slight worry she'd felt about Pip all afternoon away, too. Her sister was a big girl; if Pip needed a break from the movie, then she'd know to take it.

After Pip had made Matt a plate, Pip had gone straight to bed—pale and quiet.

Pan had used the time to finish cleaning the kitchen and to think. About her sister. And about him.

He might get under her skin, and he might be the biggest player of Masterson County, but one thing she could not deny and never would—Levi Masterson worked his ass off.

He wasn't one of those wealthy ranchers who sat back and let everyone else do the work for him. No, if there was work to be done, he was right out there doing it with them. A few times when she'd been too busy he had grabbed the broom and swept the kitchen floor when it had needed it.

He was not the least bit lazy—annoying, capable of getting under her skin, capable of making her dream things she just was not ready to deal with—but lazy, he was not. And if he got too busy, he often neglected his own needs to get things done. "Did you get everything done?"

Stupid question. Nothing was ever completely done on a ranch, especially one of this size. There was always something that still needed done.

One of the reasons why she had once dreamed of leaving Masterson County far behind. Not going too far, she guessed. Just down to a bigger city, somewhere where she could do something besides deal with cows or goats or boy children coming out her ears.

Pan didn't regret what she'd had to do since they'd lost her mother. Far from it. She had been there for her family when they had needed her, and she'd kept the family afloat financially for two years. Even though she had three older sisters, everyone had just assumed Pan would handle the money side of things, as her mother once had. And she'd done it without complaining even once. Even when she'd been so terrified she'd make a mistake and they'd lose everything.

It had taken everything she'd had to figure out a way to keep Perci in nursing school long enough for her sister to make it through. The salary Perci had brought in after that had made the only difference in their family's financial survival.

Pan would never forget the hours she'd worked cleaning toilets to get Perci through.

But she had once had her own dreams, too.

Pan made the best of the hands she'd been dealt. One of those hands had led her to right where she was. She'd make the most of it, too.

As long as Levi didn't continue to be the curve ball she didn't know how to handle. She stood and focused on the bedraggled cowboy in front of her. Levi favored his left arm, and he looked beyond exhausted. Pan fought the immediate worry that rushed through her.

She wasn't used to Levi looking like that.

Pan washed the grunge from mopping off her hands and turned back to him. "Levi, what did you do? Did you hurt yourself badly?"

"One of the bulls got a little cranky. He got my arm. Matt's dealing with him now, but he sent me back here in the hopes that Nate would be around somewhere. I don't think it's broken, but you know how older siblings are."

She grabbed a clean dishrag from the drawer and wet it. He held still and let her tend to him. Pan's hands trembled as she dealt with the blood on his arm. She bit her lip and looked up at him.

His eyes darkened and focused on her lips.

"I'm ok, baby girl. I'm meaner than the bull could ever be."

She just shook her head and continued cleaning him up. Sometimes she half thought the man needed a keeper. He may be a hard worker and out there right next to his men, but sometimes he took far too many risks for her peace of mind.

Pan had had enough of taking risks. There had been so many times over the past two years when she'd risked half the family's checking account just to pay a creditor—there had been a few times her risks hadn't paid off. They'd barely held.

She'd never forget the fear of not having enough money to feed a five-year-old. Never forget the pang of an empty stomach before bed. Never forget the fear of losing the ones she loved somehow. Never.

Pan had learned one highly valuable lesson since they'd lost their mother—how to *plan* for everything. How to make it through.

She hadn't planned on Levi, though.

She would stick to her next plan, too—as soon as she figured out what it would be.

For the last two years she'd worked so hard to see her family through and try to pay off that damn hospital. Things were finally going well for the Tylers; she just didn't know what she was going to do next. Her every thought for two years had been money and what to do next. Phoebe had been so busy with the boys and her weaving to sell, Pip with the ranch and bringing in horses for them to board, Perci had worked herself into exhaustion at the hospital to bring in every extra penny she could, just to pay down her student loans.

Just so Pan could take what money was left and do what she had to in order to feed them all and pay the damned light bill.

It was all she'd been able to focus on.

But now that was over. Money was still tight, but it wasn't nearly as bad as it had been. Joel had even hired them an attorney to fight the insurance company over the falsified accident reports from her mother's death. There was hope on the horizon. There might even one day be a chance at a real settlement.

Pressure wasn't as strong on her any longer. She had room to think about the future again.

And that meant Levi.

She didn't want to be his housekeeper forever; she didn't want to live there in the shadow of Phoebe and Pip, either. They were Mastersons now, too. It was time she had her own life, her own plan, her own path.

And whether she liked it or not, that path did not include the man in front of her.

So why was she letting him keep her so confused all the time? Not a lick of it made sense.

15

THE TWO LITTLE SCRATCHES ON HIS ARM WERE not going to kill him, but Levi stood still while she fussed. Pan had her red hair pulled back into two narrow braids.

She smelled like a mix of lemon and that indefinable scent that was her. She looked tired—that was his first thought. And no wonder. She'd been up since five making breakfast for him and the crew and then working all day with that damned movie company, then coming home and cooking and cleaning here. He checked the clock; it was almost seven, now. Had she rested at all?

She finished cleaning the mud and blood off

him, having him taken care of neatly in less than two minutes.

Levi ignored the twinge in his slightly injured arm and scooped her up. He dropped a quick kiss on her pretty lips.

"Thanks, honey."

Instead of lowering her to the floor, he carried her into the living room, despite her protests. None of his brothers or her sisters were anywhere around. For the first time in a while, they had a bit of privacy. He was going to take advantage of that.

"What are you doing?" she almost squeaked the question. Levi bit back a grin. He loved disconcerting this woman, every chance he could.

"What do you think I'm doing? I'm carrying you into the living room." He did just that, carrying her toward the large, overstuffed recliner that he'd claimed as his long ago. He sank into it and pulled the girl down onto his lap. "You look tired, sweetie. I don't want you pushing yourself so much right now. Not until that damned Bowles is finished around here. The rest of us can pitch in and help out with the cleaning and the cooking. Or I'll hire someone to help you. Would you like that?"

She looked at him like he was crazy. "You're

going to hire your housekeeper a *housekeeper?* Levi, that's insane."

But Levi had never really thought of her as his housekeeper exactly.

Well, maybe at first he had.

She had applied to his job posting and had the most experience despite her age. But after about a month of having her in his home on a regular basis something in him had shifted. He'd started to think of it less as his home, and more as *their* home. The one they'd share forever, if she would just get on board.

Joel and Matt and their wives were planning to move out soon. As soon as the renovations on their new places were done. Nate was still around, but he spent most of his time at the hospital, anyway. He was like a ghost at times.

No, this house was always intended to be Levi's. Levi's—and the woman he would one day share it with.

If he had his way, that woman was already in his arms. Levi just didn't know how to make her see that he was completely serious about how he felt about her.

"Seriously, Levi, what are you doing?"

He heard the nerves in her voice and he

smiled. He had Pan right where he wanted her for the moment. Now he was going to take the time to enjoy her.

"Do I make you nervous? You see, I think I do. And that makes me wonder why I make you so nervous. *No.* Just hold still. You really don't want to be squirming around right where you're at."

"Levi, you're such a pervert. I'm not entirely certain, but I think I could sue you for this if I wanted."

"But why would you want to? No; seriously, honey, just stay where you are for a minute. I need..."

Some of the humor left him, as he remembered exactly where he had been before hurting his arm. The bull he had lost was going to cost him a pretty chunk of change. He just hoped his brother Matt could keep the one who'd gotten Levi's arm alive.

But it was more than that. That animal shouldn't have died. He and Matt agreed on that. Levi was going to find out what had happened and soon. "I just need to hold you for a minute, honey. That's all."

Levi's arms tightened around her and pulled her as close as he could.

16

SOMETHING IN HIS VOICE HAD HAD HER stilling, right there on his lap, and looking at him. Closely for the first time. There was strain around Levi's eyes, strain she wasn't used to seeing. Something had happened out there besides his injury— something that made the usually affable and charming Levi look worried. "What's wrong?"

"I lost my bull, honey, for no logical reason. Matt's looking into it now."

She gasped. Losing a bull was a big blow to a ranch of any size. Levi's stock didn't exactly come cheap. The bull especially; it was one of the best of the best and had been purchased from the W-

Deane Ranch in Finley Creek, Texas. The strain of cattle had been developed there at the W-Deane and was greatly prized for its traits. That this one had been lost could create some serious problems for Levi.

This could be a major setback for Levi *and* her father.

Not only that, but also, like every one of his brothers, Levi was an animal lover. He cared about his stock, even those he sold for consumption. No wonder he was so unlike he normally was.

She surprised herself—and probably Levi, too —when she wrapped her arms around his neck and hugged him. He felt so warm and strong against her—she didn't like seeing him hurting. "I'm sorry. I'm sure Matt will figure out what happened."

"I've got some of the boys moving the rest of the herd away from that field just in case. I probably should get out there myself, but...there's nowhere else in the world I'd rather be than right here. With you."

This time, she didn't think the man was joking. Sometimes with him it was hard to tell, especially when he turned on the charm. Which was all the time with her—no matter who was nearby. Levi flirted with her almost constantly; she didn't sense he was flirting this time. No, this time he meant it.

His arms tightened around her. Pan did not push him away.

17

Levi rocked her, forcing himself to keep his hands in neutral territory. The woman was completely innocent after all. He wasn't about to do something to hurt her. Or scare her. Not his girl. He fiddled with the end of one red-gold braid and forced himself to ignore the press of small feminine curves to his chest.

It had been a long time since he had a woman on his lap like this. That it was her made it all the more difficult for him to keep his hands in neutral territory.

Levi wasn't an animal, after all; his mother had raised him better than that. "So what's your schedule like tomorrow?"

"I get a break until two. Pip and Matt are on most of the morning, though. I figure to take care of things around here, then drive to Mrs. Carson's and handle her place. I may have time to do a second place tomorrow, too. If I'm fast enough here."

He frowned. Mrs. Carson's place was clear across the county and not exactly easily accessible. There was a lot of remote areas between this place and that place. Anything could happen to her.

"You taking one your sisters with you?"

She shook her head lightly. "No, they're all busy. I may take Parker with me; he likes Mrs. Carson's old donkey. He doesn't have any scenes tomorrow or the next day like the rest of my brothers. I may bring him back here and let him spend the night with me."

"Why don't you let me or one of the hands drive you? Your fan belt has been squealing, and I've been meaning to tell you. I want to take a look at it. Make sure it's not about ready to go. I'd hate for you and Parker to get stuck halfway to Mrs. Carson's." He tried to keep himself from just pulling her right up against him. He had to be content with the fact that she wasn't squirming to get off his lap yet. Pan wasn't one he could rush. He knew that.

Too bad his hormones didn't seem to have gotten the message.

"Levi...I can take care of myself. It's not your job to take care of my car. If there's something wrong with that that I can't fix it myself, I'll ask my father."

"Your father's on his way down to Finley Creek. I think he'll be there for a day or two. Trying to figure out what's happening with the bulls. And that makes you my responsibility. Because I want to make you my responsibility." Damn, did he want that.

He wanted the legal right to care about this woman.

He was ready for just that.

Too bad Pandora wasn't.

"I don't want to be your responsibility, though. I want to be my own responsibility, and that's it."

The resolve in her tone made it very clear that she meant it. And things were going to get a bit harder for him.

"I understand that. I was the same way until I realized I liked having people care about me and caring about them. If you'd let me, Pandora Claire, I'll take good care of you."

18

SHE DIDN'T THINK HE JUST MEANT HER CAR. And that was what terrified her the most about him. Pan didn't know if she could trust that; his interest could wane if she gave him what he wanted. Levi had dated half the available women in the county, after all.

Pan wasn't interested in being a number—especially with him. Not him.

So why hadn't she climbed off the man's lap yet?

"Listen, Masterson, I know what you're after. The entire county knows what you're after. And I'll not play that game. I never have, and I never will. When I do get involved with a guy, it's going to be on my terms. And it will be serious. Have you ever been serious about a woman in your entire life?" She wasn't being confrontational or antagonistic or anything. She couldn't be at the moment. Pan honestly needed to know. Because where she was sitting felt seriously...serious.

Right.

Almost too easy.

And *that* terrified her.

She didn't want Levi to be so...easy.

"Yes. Since about a month after you started living here. I haven't even thought about another woman since."

"So less than six months? Not exactly a track record. In case you missed it, we've not been together six months, Levi. We've not been together at all. I don't believe in insta-love."

"What the hell is *insta-love*? There was nothing instant about the way I felt about you. I mean, it took a while. It probably started that day Tom Rutherford nearly killed Phoebe and Joel. You look so fierce standing on the porch protecting your little brothers. I just wanted to scoop you right up and promise to always keep you safe. No matter what I had to do. Your eyes. I still dream about your eyes that day, honey. What's so wrong with that? I don't know where you get the idea that I'm not serious about how I feel, Pandora. Because I am damned serious. You're not exactly the kind of woman a man trifles with, if he's not. Not to mention the fact that if I do something you don't like, all you have to do is tell my own brothers. They will beat the shit out of me. And they are bigger than me!"

Hard hands tightened around her waist, and he shifted her until her eyes met his. Never had she seen him quite so serious. "Listen to me, Pandora Claire. Just listen to me. I have *never* felt this way about a woman—not the way I feel about you. Just keep that in mind, when you're off kissing movie stars and flirting with big-time billionaire directors. You make me feel something more than I ever thought possible. You have ruined me. Now you have to fix what you've broken. Before you ruin me completely, forever. Don't make me suffer, please?"

What sane woman would ever turn a man like him away? Not when he was holding her right there on his lap, telling her that he had feelings for her? Pan fought the shiver that went through her.

She was not about to let him ruin her plans, but she couldn't force herself to move away from him at that moment. It seemed harder to move away than it was to get closer. It just seemed easier to stay right where she was.

And when he leaned his head down her lips were already open and waiting for him.

When he pulled back for air, one thing was infinitely clear to her.

Hunter Clark couldn't hold a candle to the rancher kissing her right now.

19

SHE DID TAKE HER YOUNGEST BROTHER WITH her, and he enjoyed playing in the woman's backyard. Mrs. Carson was a retired grandmother who'd once worked as a schoolteacher. At one time, Pan and her sisters had attended the local elementary school—mostly to get four young girls out from underfoot while her parents worked the ranch. Mrs. Carson had been her teacher until her parents had made the decision that the school was just too far away and that they needed the girls home. She thought Mrs. Carson enjoyed hearing Parker's tales of making a movie almost as much as her younger brother enjoyed telling them. Still, by the time she was done cleaning

Mrs. Carson's place she was more than ready to go home.

It was getting ready to storm. She had intended to get at least one other place done for the day, but that wasn't going to happen. She'd been hoping to speak with the client about giving her a reference to use with the Preston family. They were the most well-to-do family in the greater Masterson County area, even more so than Levi and his brothers. If she cleaned for them at least once a week, it would beef up her savings enough that she might actually be able to afford to replace her car soon.

Or at least get it tuned up. Because Levi was right. There was something wrong with her fan belt now.

She didn't really have enough money to spend on fixing it; she hadn't been going to tell him that there were some things he just didn't need to worry about.

She wasn't going to let him feel responsible for her; she wasn't about to start depending on him, either. Pan wasn't going to let that man get under her skin any more than he already had.

She knew exactly what she *wasn't* going to do with Levi, at least.

Damn him. Pan just didn't know how she was going to deal with the way he made her *feel*. Short of running up into the mountains that lined the back of Levi's property. Running. Tylers didn't *run*.

Parker chattered at her as she drove the forty miles back toward the Masterson place. Her little brother was significantly cute and always had been. He'd been born when she was fourteen, and she'd spent a lot of time helping care for him. She and her sisters had taken turns helping their mother with him and the other young children after their mother had given birth to Parker.

She missed living with her brothers, and she wouldn't deny that. It wasn't that she didn't see them as much, because she did.

It just didn't *feel* the same.

She sighed. That was the way things happened, right? You wanted change, then when you got it you missed everything from before.

Pan hated feeling this confused.

And most of it was Levi's fault. That man...she just couldn't stop thinking about him.

"Are you sad today?" her little brother asked.

"No, not really. Why do you ask?"

"You have that face again."

Parker crunched up his face in a way that made her laugh.

"Do I?"

"Yes. It's the one you have when you are thinking. Or sad. I don't like it when my Pan is sad." He shot her a chiding look—for a moment looking just like their mother. And her. She and Parker really favored the mother she missed every day.

"I'm not really feeling sad today, Park. Just a little tired and lots to think about."

"Like Levi. I know. I heard, you know."

Levi. Again. She just couldn't escape him, could she? "What did you hear?"

"Daddy and Perci. Perci thinks he's really cute, but he's not serious. Daddy thinks he is serious. And that he loves *loves* you."

"They do, do they?" It didn't surprise her that her father and her sister had been discussing her and Levi. It seemed like everyone everywhere was. Even Mrs. Carson had had good things to say about 'Pandora's young man.'

Like they were inevitable, or something. Like Perci and Nate were, too. Mrs. Carson had had a lot to say about that fine young doctor her sister had 'caught.'

Urgh. Like they were men-fish or something.

"A few days ago. When Mr. Clark asked Perci if you were dating anyone."

"Oh? Mr. Clark, from the movie?"

"Yep. He was talking to Daddy about the horses and about you and Perci and Pip and Phoebe. And how pretty and nice you all were. Perci and me were in the barn. But then she took Skye outside. Perci told him that you weren't dating anyone; Daddy told him that you kind of were. I think Daddy likes Levi. I do. He's going to take me fishing, you know."

"Again?" Levi had taken her brother fishing before. She'd watched him and little boy walked down to the pond from Levi's kitchen window. It had struck her, not for the first time, just how beautiful Levi was. How kind.

Parker and Patton both admired him. Liked him. Actually wanted to spend time with him—and not just Matt and Joel.

Levi was just...a part of everything now. Easy.

Except for her.

"He said anytime I wanted. He's like my big brother now, too. You know? Even though Matt's married to Pip and Joel's married to Phoebe, Levi said he gets to be my brother, too. A guy could never have too many brothers. I think you can have too many sisters sometimes, though."

"Parker, which one of us would you get rid of?"

Her youngest brother just grinned.

Pan was still laughing when the large, dark SUV pulled out in front of her and slammed on its brakes.

Pan cursed. She jerked the wheel to the left, sending her little car careening into the ditch. Just before her head slammed into the steering wheel, she reached out with her right arm and did her best to hold her little brother in place. She tried to protect him as much she could as the airbag deployed. He was just so small.

Then Pan felt nothing but white-hot pain followed by blackness.

20

LEVI HAD JUST FINISHED HIS PHONE CALL WITH his partner in Texas. Thankfully, Travis Deane was a reasonable man who understood situations happened. Still, both he and Deane had had high hopes for this particular bull in their little study. That the animal had died with no explanation didn't make a bit of sense. He was feeling that frustration when the phone rang again.

Levi almost didn't answer until he saw her number on the caller ID. Pan didn't call him often and only when something was wrong. His instincts flared.

"Honey," he breathed into the phone after he answered it. "What's wrong?"

"Levi?" a little voice definitely not Pandora's said. "It's Parker, Levi. You need to come get us right now. The car crashed, and Pan won't wake up. I don't know what I'm supposed to do. And my head hurts. Come get us. I can't get Daddy to answer his phone."

"Parker, son, where are you? Did you have a car wreck?" Levi was already moving toward the door.

"The big black car did not wait their turn and almost hit us. We hit a big rock instead, and now Pan won't wake up. She won't wake up. I don't want her to go to heaven in the car like Mommy did. You'll come get us, won't you?"

"Parker, were you at Mrs. Carson's today?" Levi ran toward the front door; he heard a car pull in. He prayed it was Nate, but would settle for Matt, or Joel. Any of the three could help him and fast.

"Yes. But we had just...I can see Ryan Hobson's house. But nobody is home today. I tried to get them to help." The little boy was sobbing now, and it took Levi a moment to understand what he'd said. But it was the information he needed. The Hobsons lived closer to the Mastersons than they did the Carsons. She wasn't that far away.

Matt was climbing out of his truck when Levi came running. Levi pulled the phone away from his mouth and yelled at his brother to get the engine started.

Matt didn't hesitate. Levi climbed into the passenger seat and grabbed Matt's phone out of his brother's hand. Matt turned the key. Levi spoke into his own cell again. Matt was smart; he'd catch on quick. "Parker, I'm going to have to put my phone down. I'm going to call Joel with Matt's phone, ok? I want you to stay on my phone until I get there. We're going to come help? You're not alone, I promise. We're coming. You stay with Pan, understand?"

He dialed the sheriff as fast as he could and explained to the dispatcher exactly what was going on. But he knew the truth; he and Matt would probably get there long before an ambulance did—because Masterson County was just too damned big sometimes.

21

If it had been anyone other than one of those damned Tylers, she would've stopped the car and offered help, but those Tylers supposedly took care of themselves.

Viv kept going.

Besides, she didn't need the hassle of dealing with Pan Tyler or Levi's brother the sheriff tonight. Viv had a lot to think about, with the news her father had delivered. He was dying. Sooner than she had expected. Nothing was going to change that. If she wanted to keep her hands on the damned ranch she despised, she was going to have to find a man capable of running it for her.

Viv knew the man she wanted. She just had to

find a way to get him away from that damn Pan Tyler in order to make that happen.

For a moment, she wished Pan were dead. That would make things so much simpler for her.

But Viv hadn't missed the little boy climbing out of the passenger seat after the little red car had swerved off the road. It wasn't exactly a fair thing to do to a kid, and he hadn't been very old. She thought that was the youngest boy, and he was all of seven or eight. No. She didn't want the girl dead. Just as far away from Levi as Viv could get her.

22

Levi barely let Matt stop the truck before he jumped free and started running toward Pan's little red two-door. The car sat at a terrifying angle. Six inches more, and it would've flipped on its front end. But it hadn't. Thank God, it hadn't.

Parker was still crying, blood covering the hair the same color as his sister's. Levi squeezed the boy's shoulder quickly as he ran by the crying child toward the front of the car. Matt was only steps behind him.

Matt had grabbed his bag from his truck, where he carried the basics of first aid. Matt was only a vet, but he was more medical care than was otherwise available. Levi just hoped it was enough.

Her door stood open, and he could see her, see the blood coating her head. She wasn't moving. For a moment he thought she was gone.

He yelled her name, cursed, or something, he wasn't entirely certain. And then those Tyler blue eyes of hers opened.

Levi said a prayer of thanks quickly as he stumbled down the ditch closer to his girl. "Pandora Claire, honey. Just how bad are you hurt?"

"What happened?" she tried to move, but Matt wouldn't let her.

"Don't really know, darlin'; let's just worry about getting you out of there first, ok? Now I couldn't find the doctor right away, but I did find the vet. And since you're a bit on the stubborn as a mule side, I figured you wouldn't mind. You just stay still, and let Matt take a look at you, ok? Then we'll get you out of there, take you over to see Nate and Perci. We'll go see if they're fighting again today. How does that sound?"

Pan didn't answer, out again. He turned to his brother. "I need to get her out of there."

He saw the understanding and compassion in his brother's eyes. "I don't know, Levi. But her pulse is steady. She seems to be breathing ok. I think our best bet is to just leave her where she's at until the ambulance arrives. I don't want to make the situation worse by moving her if we shouldn't. We don't have the necessary equipment to keep her from hurting herself worse if I'm wrong."

Levi hunkered down next to her, kneeling in the dirt beside the open door. Her left hand hung limp at her side, and he carefully wrapped his fingers around hers and prayed.

He'd known he cared a great deal about this woman, but just how much hadn't been entirely clear to him until that very moment.

Her little brother cuddled up next to his side, and Levi wrapped his arm around the boy who looked so much like her and just held him while they waited.

23

There was a demon cracking her skull open with a sledgehammer when Pan opened her eyes. People were around here everywhere. Two men and a woman, and they were trying to get her out of her car. There was something around her neck, and they were strapping her down. She fought immediate panic.

"It's ok, honey. I've got you. You're going to be fine, remember? We're just being extra careful. Letting Joel's boys and the EMTs practice on you. That's all."

"Levi. You're here." How had he gotten there? The last thing she remembered, she and Parker had been at Mrs. Carson's...Parker...she'd had

Parker with her. "Levi! Where's Parker? Where is he?"

"Hey, hey, hey. Parker's just fine. Matt's got him now. They're going to follow you and me. We're going to take a ride in the helicopter."

No. She knew exactly how much that cost—even with insurance. "Levi...can't afford..."

"You can't. But I can. And I'm going to take care of you."

She wanted to argue, but her entire body hurt just too much to even think about it. Tears leaked from her eyes.

Levi was right there next to her. She wanted to reach for him, but her arms wouldn't work. Pan just kept her eyes on his as long as she could. He was right there.

And that was where he stayed. Pan forced herself to breathe, forced herself not to panic.

Parker was safe. And Levi was right there with her. She finally let go and allowed the darkness to take her. Just for a little while...

24

LEVI FOUGHT THE URGE TO PANIC AS THEY strapped her to the backboard and carried her to the waiting emergency helicopter. The ambulance was clear across the county. No one had been willing to wait to get Pan the help she needed, least of all him, Joel, or Matt.

No one questioned that Levi would be the one riding with her, either. Matt would bring Parker. Nate and the rest of the hospital was already waiting for her.

He kept his fingers around hers and kept his body out of the paramedics' paths.

Levi just stayed close to her head, kept her

small fingers in his, and wished he knew how to make her better.

The paramedics were hooking her up to fluids and checking her vitals, everything he didn't understand.

"She's stable, Levi," a paramedic Levi had known for years said. "Just took a knock to the head that's keeping her out of it."

"She's so small, Jake." Levi took a good long look at her. "And she's hurt and..."

"You can't fix it. Trust me: I know." Jake's attention strayed to the female paramedic. She had been a few years behind them in school. The woman was hooking Pan up to an IV, calm and steady in spite of the bumpy flight. "We'll get her to the hospital in the next ten minutes. She'll be in good hands once Nate takes over. If not him, Dr. Jacobi is on tonight. She's good at what she does. Everyone at the hospital is. Pan'll be ok."

Levi appreciated his friend's attempt to make him feel better, but he wasn't going to stop worrying until he got to talk to his brother.

And until Pan opened those blue eyes and looked at him again.

25

When Pan opened her eyes again, she was in the midst of the ER and a Masterson brother leaned over her. It wasn't the one she wanted, though he was equally as handsome. Perci stood at Nate's side. Pan reached for her sister with her right hand. Her left was tied down to something when she pulled on it. "Perci...Parker?"

"He's coming in with Matt, Pan. I'll keep him here until Phoebe and Pip and the others arrive." Perci brushed the hair off her forehead gently. "We're just going to take care of you right now."

"Well, at least the two of you have finally stopped arguing." Pan closed her eyes against the glare of the fluorescent lights.

Perci was there. Nate was there.

And Levi...she opened her eyes again. Levi.

He was right there next to her, his face pale and his eyes wide with worry. With fear. She pulled her hand from Perci's and reached toward him instead.

He'd come for her, hadn't he? "Levi...how did you know I was hurt?"

"Parker called me, honey. Seems he thought I needed to rescue you." Levi covered her shoulder with those strong fingers of his. He felt warm and real and safe right there next to her.

She was with people who loved her now. She was safe.

And her head was about to crack open. Pan closed her eyes once again, his name on her lips.

26

IT TOOK OVER TWELVE HOURS FOR HER TO finally be able to think long enough to put two and two together and end up with four. Pan had gotten lucky, though. Only a concussion, a cracked rib, and a sprained wrist where she'd held Parker in place on impact. The car had almost been too old for an airbag. He'd come away with only bruises from his seatbelt and the airbag's deployment. Her car was a leftover from her parents' years before and had had no backseat. Otherwise he would have been in the backseat and probably not as bruised. But he seemed to be ok when Perci snuck him back into the hospital room to visit her.

"You, Parker Owen, are my hero. Come here." She held out her uninjured arm to this little brother that looked the most like her. "That was really smart, calling Levi like that."

"Levi loves you like Matt loves my Pip. I knew he'd rescue you."

"I don't know about that." She winced when she thought about it. No doubt Levi was attracted to her, and cared about her, and she definitely hadn't forgotten what he'd said after he'd kissed her, but love?

She most definitely wasn't ready to think about *love* with Levi Masterson. But she had to admit that when she'd first opened her eyes that morning, she had half looked around for him.

Perci leaned over her. "Nate forced Levi to go home about two hours ago. Something was mentioned about him possibly showering and sleeping for a while. I told him that I would stand guard over you, along with Park, until Phoebe and Pip arrive to take over for me."

"You all don't have to babysit me. There are things that need to be getting done." She loved her family, and knew why they were going to be there. They were Tylers and Tylers took care of their own. No matter what. But Pan really hated people fussing over her. "Anyone called Dad?"

"That rancher in Finley Creek has a friend with a private jet. He's flying Dad home as we speak."

"But..."

"No buts, Pandora. You opened the box with this one. Scared us all really good." Perci settled Parker in the chair by the window with her cell phone. She'd started carrying it after everything that had happened to Pip and Phoebe over the last several months. Parker was fascinated by cell phones. "What happened?"

"A black truck or something. They pulled out right in front of me. I had to jerk the wheel to get us out of the way."

"Did you recognize who it was? They just left you two there. Joel's trying to find them. Charge them with leaving the scene or something."

"No. But it all happened fast, and I was worried about Parker being in the passenger seat."

"He's fine, Pan. I promise. I checked him again myself this morning. And he spent the night with Phoebe and Pip. Nate checked him out before breakfast. You were the one to take the hardest knock." Perci leaned over and checked the stitches in her forehead. "I think you're going to end up with a scar just like mine and Pip's. Right between your eyes, probably. You always were trying to copy us. Don't ever scare us like that again. You might really annoy the tar out of me, but I love you, you goob."

"Love you, too. So when am I getting out of here?"

"Tomorrow at the earliest," a male voice said from the door. She turned her aching head to the side slightly. Levi's older brother stood there, looking all handsome and massive. Nate was the biggest Masterson brother, though he really did resemble Levi—if she squinted, which thanks to her headache was a requirement of survival. "Levi will come for you at noon."

"Why Levi and not someone else? I know he has a lot to handle right now."

Nate smiled. He really was beautiful; she didn't quite understand why Perci called him the devil personified most times. "There isn't any-where else he wants to be. You know how he is."

"Relentless." And the last time she had wak-ened in the middle of the night, he had been right there in the chair now occupied by her baby brother. Every time she had needed him he had been right there.

And she had looked for him, instinctively. Because a part of her had known Levi would be right where she needed him.

27

SHE WAS HURTING, AND ALL LEVI WANTED TO do was scoop her up and carry her inside the main house—and straight to his bed, where she belonged. But he restrained himself.

But one thing was definitely clear—she wasn't about to hide herself away in her little garage apartment where she went to escape him at night. Nope. Pandora Claire was going to be in the main house where he and her sisters could keep an eye on her.

When he told her that, she didn't even protest. That told him all he needed to know. He carried her into his house and just wished he could hold her like that forever.

LEVI SLIPPED FROM THE BED FOR THE THIRD time. He just needed to see her for himself. Every time he had drifted off, Pan's little red car would flash through his dreams, reminding him of how she had looked, so hurt and defenseless.

It was going to be a long time before that image would be erased from his head.

The guest room she slept in was right next to his. He stepped closer to the bed and just stared at her for a while, reminding himself that she was right there in front of him and safe. Levi straightened the covers over her and started back toward his own room where he belonged before he did something totally stupid.

28

Pan knew who stood next to her bed, and she forced herself to breathe. What she wanted to do was roll over on her back and look at him. Have him hold her again; keep the nightmares at bay.

Her mother had died in a car accident. Perci and their brother Phoenix had also almost died in that wreck. Not only could she not forget what had happened to her, but the grief for her mother was incredibly strong at the moment.

Life had been so much easier before they'd lost her mother.

Levi was almost at the door. In that instant, the last thing she wanted him to do was leave.

"Levi?"

He jerked around. "Did I wake you, honey?"

"I don't know. I haven't slept all that great anyway. What are you doing here?"

"Checking on you."

"Oh." She didn't know what to say to a man in her bedroom. It was definitely not something she had ever experienced before. "I'm sore, but I'll be ok."

"I know. I just...you scared me today." He walked back to the bed and just stood there. Pan pulled the blankets closer, then reached out with one hand and flipped on the lamp.

He wore thin gray shorts, and the rest of him was completely bare.

Levi took perfect cowboy body to the extremes. She had never noticed a man's chest quite the same way before. A small thin line of dark hair ran down his abs and the fingers on her uninjured hand actually curled. She wanted to touch him.

She wanted to touch.

Pan didn't know if it was because she was sore and vulnerable and it was hard to keep on the plan or because it was something about him. Because something in her had changed.

The one thing she really remembered about the accident was opening her eyes and seeing him.

He'd been right there, and things hadn't seemed quite so terrifying.

Or maybe she had only been dreaming that.

"I scared me, too." What was she supposed to say now? Levi sank down onto the bed next to her, sending her rolling toward his greater weight.

He felt so warm, so real. The fingers of her uninjured hand were on top of the blanket. Levi wrapped his hand around hers. "I'm glad you're here with me, honey. I'm sorry if I woke you up. In my head I know you're ok, but as soon as I close my eyes..."

"Yeah. Thank you. For being out there. Whenever I think of Parker out there, being so scared like that...he's still nervous in a car anyway because of what happened to our mother. This...I should have seen the other car faster."

"Hey! Not your fault. Parker said the black car was just there out of nowhere. You're both safe now." He turned slightly, still holding her fingers. "And I finally got you right where I want you."

"What?"

He grinned that trademark Levi Masterson grin. "I have you in my lair, honey. Maybe not in my bed exactly, but close enough. I'm going to work on moving you a few yards down the hall—

toward my room, though, not Nate's. Eventually, I'll get you on my sheets. They're silk."

"I know what your sheets are made of—I changed them yesterday morning. I'm not interested in being the latest Levi Masterson conquest." Levi liked women—everyone in the county knew it. Pan couldn't be just a passing thing to him. She just...couldn't.

"Honey, you are not some conquest. You never will be. Like I said before, I haven't even thought about another woman since that day we almost lost Phoebe and Joel. I haven't been able to."

"Why?" That day had been horrible, terrifying. One of the worst ones in her adult life. If he hadn't been there with her and the boys she would have fractured into millions of pieces. He had just been there.

And she hadn't been able to shake him since.

"Hell, I don't know. You certainly aren't an easy woman. You're really quite contrary." He pulled her hand up to his mouth and kissed her palm lightly. "Most women are a bit more manageable."

She laughed when he grinned at her. "Levi, you're an idiot."

"Over you, yes." He tucked her hand back

under the blanket, then waggled his eyebrows at her. "Love the outfit, honey. That one of Nate's T-shirts?"

"Yes." She tried not to blush, but all she had on was his brother's shirt. Phoebe had snagged it for her from the fresh laundry Pan had left on the counter in the laundry room. Her sisters hadn't even helped her into fresh underwear. She was practically as naked as she could get.

"Hmmm. No—on second thought, I think it's mine. Nate has a similar one, but his has blue lettering. My shirt, my lair, my woman. I like that. Symmetrical and all." He toyed with the soft cotton sleeve, those long warm fingers of his brushing her skin lightly.

"Go away." No. Don't go. Stay. Pan didn't quite know what she wanted at the moment. "I'm not your woman. It doesn't work that way."

"Of course, it does. I'm a Masterson. You're a Tyler. We're kind of a given. Or don't you listen to town gossip?"

"That is all your fault. And I still haven't forgiven you." He'd told his friends she was off limits once. And they'd all just run with the idea. Some had even teased her about it. At the grocery store, the mechanic—who was a Tyler cousin, the gas station, people everywhere had just acted like she was Levi's girl. Because he had said she was.

Never mind the fact that she wasn't interested in dating anyone at the moment—they'd all just believed him when he'd said the two of them had something going.

A woman wanted a choice.

And the idiot had yet to apologize for embarrassing her like that. She strongly suspected Levi never would. Because he was unrepentant.

He rolled back on the bed, quickly slipping under the blanket next to her. He rested his head on her pillow—but kept his hands to himself mostly. One might have strayed, a little. Pan wasn't totally sure.

"You will eventually. I'm kind of cute. Or so I've been told."

Levi pulled the quilt up around her shoulders, then brushed his fingers through her hair. "One little kiss and then I'll leave you alone. For the rest of the night."

"You're getting up in an hour to go milk Bessie."

"So give me a snuggle before I have to go out into the cold."

"I washed your thermal underwear yesterday.

I think you'll be just fine." They sounded so stupidly domestic, didn't they? Pan wanted to fight that idea—but she also just wanted to cuddle up next to him.

"How about at least a hug? Something to help chase the nightmares away?" One hand snuck around her waist and practically scorched her skin. One mostly bare leg slid alongside hers. He scooted closer, and then he was right there, wrapped around her. Pan felt every hard muscle of him pressed against her. She shivered.

He felt so hot against her. She hadn't expected him to put out so much literal heat. Nor had she expected to want to just curl up like a cat next to him. To just...snuggle.

Pandora Claire Tyler never snuggled up to men. Period. So what made this one so different? So much of a plan-wrecker?

She didn't have a clue. But Pan couldn't seem to force herself to make him let her go. Her body relaxed against his and she pressed closer. Or maybe he did. She wasn't certain, and what did it matter, really? No one but the two of them were ever going to know what happened between them in this bed. Unless she told them. Or he did. Which she somehow doubted he ever would.

His arms were strong around her, warm and safe, and exactly what she needed.

He brushed his lips against her forehead. "Go back to sleep. I'll just hold you for a while. Just for a while. You can go back to resisting me in the morning."

"It is morning, Levi."

"Is it? Then go back to sleep, and I'll take care of everything today."

Pan did just that, snuggled against his chest. Like it was easy or something.

When had Levi become so easy?

29

LEVI HELD HER UNTIL THE SUN PEEKED through the window and he heard his brother's footsteps. Nate stuck his head in the room, then snorted when he saw Levi wrapped around the sleeping woman. "You're just as pathetic as the other two."

"No. I'm just as brilliant as the other two. You're the one who can't get two brain cells together to see what—who—is right in front of your face." Levi didn't want to take his hands off her, but like it or not, he had work to do. And his girl was out; he could feel her light breath brushing against his neck. He hadn't meant to slide into the bed with her, but it had just happened. He wouldn't regret it. "If you were as smart as Mama always claimed, you'd have already gotten Perci to look beyond your ugly face. Instead you just snip at the poor girl all the time."

Levi slipped from the bed then tucked the blanket tight around Pan. She hummed in her sleep and snuggled back down into the spot he'd just left. It wasn't a very big bed; he definitely hadn't slept. No, he just laid there and held her.

"I'll handle Persephone as I see fit."

"Why do you call her that? No one else does."

"Oh? Rather like Pandora Claire there?" Nate asked, his usual morning grumble out in full force. He stepped further into the room. "I came by to check on her—and get your sorry ass. Did you forget that Tyler was bringing back that guy from Texas with him today to see the bulls in the north barn?"

"Hell no, I didn't forget. It's just..." He looked back at where Pan still slept, oblivious to the two men in the room with her. "Hell, Nate, I just...hell. What's a guy supposed to do?"

"What is it about Tylers that makes the three of you act like total fools? Did you really come in here and climb in bed with our housekeeper?"

"It wasn't like that. Well...mostly. We...I just

checked on her, she was awake, and we started talking. She just fell back asleep an hour ago. And I stayed." He didn't know why he felt so awkward. He'd certainly had women in his bed before— sometimes in the same house as his brothers. They knew he was no saint where the opposite sex was involved. Because it was her— that's why it mattered. He would never want anyone thinking less of her. "I'm not going to do anything to hurt her, Nate. I'm not a dog."

"No. But she's one of the damned Tylers. You can't pull your usual stuff with Phoebe and Pip's younger sister."

"I'm not pulling anything. At least nothing Joel and Matt haven't already pulled."

"Shit. You're that serious about her?"

"Yes." With every breath he took, he was growing more and more serious about that woman. "Why doesn't anyone believe me about that?"

"Because you've never been serious before?" Nate just shook his head and half snarled. Levi was used to it. His brother was constant cranky the first thing in the morning. "What are you going to do about it?"

"I don't have a damned clue."

But it gave him something to think about as he hurriedly showered and dressed.

Pan's father would be there within the hour, bringing with him the guy responsible for breeding the bull that had formed the basis of Levi's experimental herd. He still had some frozen semen to continue his early work on the herd, but if there was something genetically wrong with the bull that had caused this, then he wasn't about to pass it on. Not until he and Deane had time to figure out the answers. This was too important of a meeting for him to miss, no matter how much he wanted to stay and take care of Pan.

Levi would just deal with Deane then send the Texan on his way. And hurry back to Pan.

He checked on her once before he headed outside, but she was still sound asleep. He was covering her up again—apparently Pan liked to kick the covers off—when the door to the guestroom open, and another small redhead walked in. For a moment he thought it was his sister-in-law Pip, until he saw the scar over the left eyebrow. Pip's was over her right. "Hey Perci; I didn't hear you pull up."

"I'm on my way into the hospital, but I thought I'd check on Pan first."

"Your Daddy is on his way here soon. I figured to check on her myself before heading out to meet him."

"I have about an hour before I have to leave. I'll stick around. You go play rancher. I'll play nurse with my baby sister."

She leaned over her sister and stared at Pan for a moment. Then she checked her pulse and did other nurse-y stuff, before nodding. "Just another knock on the hardest melon ever. I think she'll be just fine."

"That's what I told them," a male voice said from the hallway. Nate was there, his habitual look of irritation on the face so like Levi father's. Nate, more than any of the other brothers, resembled the best man Levi had ever known. "Aren't you on the schedule for this morning?"

Levi watched her chin go up. She certainly looked like her sister when she did that. Pan was just as stubborn. "I switched with Jaicie. She took the early morning shift, so I could spend some time with my sister. Is that ok with you?"

"When you're ready to leave, I'll drive you in. You can pick up your car here this evening. No doubt, you'll be back here to check on her tonight. You might as well save the gas."

Levi hid a snicker. His brother had it bad and was stupid for not trying to do something about it. Perci was just as fascinating—well maybe not quite as fascinating—as Pan. His brother was an idiot for fighting the inevitable.

The truth was, the four Tyler women had been practically custom-made for the Masterson men. Every moment Levi's brother spent fighting it, was one more moment that he wasn't with his girl. Nate was the only one missing out. His brother would eventually figure it out; Nate was supposed to be the smartest of them all. It was just a matter of time. In the meantime, Levi had things he needed to take care of.

30

Pan's father was four inches shorter than Levi, ripcord lean, with coloring similar to all of his daughters.

He was one hell of a guy, who worked hard for his family. First thing Phil asked after the helicopter had deposited him and his guests in the middle of the front lawn was about his youngest son and his youngest daughter. The front lawn was the only place that had the land, thanks to the damn movie crew everywhere. Levi filled him in quickly.

The man Phil had brought back with him was around Levi's age and size. A gorgeous blond woman stood next to Deane. Levi took a moment to appreciate. Before Pan, this was the type of woman who would have caught his attention. Before Pan. Beautiful, most definitely—but he preferred stubborn strawberry blondes with Tyler blue eyes.

Deane apologized for the bull's sudden death, getting straight to business in a way Levi appreciated.

"To be honest, at this point were not sure what happened. My brother—he's a vet—couldn't find any definitive answer. We don't know if it was natural causes or not."

"We'll send off samples for genetic testing. This line of cattle needs to be genetically sound before they're sent out into the world." Deane prided himself on his reputation, same as Levi. It was obvious. He was glad Phil had mentioned Deane's experimental work to him a few months ago. Even with this setback, he didn't regret it.

"Why don't you all come inside? We'll give Phil a chance to check on his kids, and get you all something to drink," he said, after they'd inspected the three other bulls from Deane's line.

"I spoke with Pip this morning, Levi. She said her sister did well through the night," Phil said.

"She was awake a few times, but I checked on

her myself a little while ago. Just a concussion, or so Nate promises me."

Levi didn't miss the confusion on the Texans' faces. "Phil's daughter Pandora and his youngest son, Parker, were in a bit of a fender bender yesterday. Parker's fine, but Pan took a hard knock to the head. She's resting inside."

Phil patted Levi on the shoulder. "Thanks again, Levi. For being there when I needed you."

"If I have my way, I always will be. It's your daughter that's proving mighty stubborn."

The blond woman looked at Levi. "So you are one of his sons-in-law?"

"No. My brothers Joel and Matt are Phil's sons-in-law. I'm not one *yet*. Pan's proving mighty stubborn in that regard. It's a Tyler female trait."

Deane laughed—loudly. "I think it's just a beautiful woman trait."

His fine fiancé just smirked at him. "Don't we have some business to attend to? I'm not sure how long Marc and the kids can deal with Horace."

Deane smiled back at her, obviously beyond gone. Lucky bastard. Levi glanced back toward the house, just as a pretty strawberry blonde walked out the back door—a laundry basket in her hands. He frowned. "Yes, ma'am. Business it is, as soon as I talk to her about taking it easy today."

Phil laughed. "Son, that's going to be a losing battle. She's just as stubborn as her mother ever was. Pan's more like my wife than any of the others."

"Obstinate woman is going to be the death of me."

Deane slapped him on the shoulder and grinned at his own woman. "I know exactly how you feel."

"Can it, Worthington, or I'll feed you to the cows."

"See? She totally loves me."

Levi barely heard their words—his entire focus was on his own girl. She should still be curled up in bed, resting. Not cleaning his damned house and folding his underwear.

31

SHE WAS OUT THERE AGAIN. PAN. SHE WAS actually hanging out laundry on a line. It had been a long time since he'd seen a woman do that. John couldn't help but stay right where he was and watch her. He had to admit Tyler women were damned fine.

Tom's wife Sadie used to hang the laundry on the line. Before she had died.

At the hands of Phoenix Tyler. He would never forget that. John stayed where he was, and just watched Phoenix's sister. The binoculars he'd found in the shed weren't the best, but he used them to keep himself entertained. He had to do something; all those hours, after all.

He was getting itchy again, he needed a fix. There were only a few places that he could get what he needed. And he had to do it at night.

Viv always had what he needed. If he could somehow get to her.

He'd sent her a text from a prepaid cell phone, but she was out of town. She'd be back tomorrow, and then he'd get what he needed.

While he waited, he would just watch those Tylers and Mastersons and imagine what it was he'd do to make them pay for all that they had taken from him.

He watched for the longest time, first as she argued with that rancher, then as that Masterson brother actually helped her with the laundry.

Masterson must want in her pants real bad in order to do women's work like that.

John had never hung laundry out in his life.

Masterson didn't have any sense of pride, did he?

John smirked as he wiped at the streak of dirt riding high on his own cheek. He hoped Viv got back real soon.

32

HUNTER GOT THE NEWS THAT HIS SCENE HAD been rescheduled due to Pan being in an accident ten minutes after he arrived at the Masterson ranch.

Instead, Bowles was going to film using some of the extras he'd hired from around the county. From the sheer number of redheads in that group, he suspected a lot of them were Tylers. Tylers were so distinctive, after all.

One of them ran in front of him, practically tripping over his feet. She was taller than Pan and her sisters, but not by much. She may have only been a year or two older, but it was hard to tell. All the Tyler women were hard to figure out when it came to age. Bowles had certainly found a family that resembled the fairies that were so important in this damned script. Blue eyes looked up at him from behind thick glasses.

Oh, this one was a sweet one, all right. Hunter didn't remember her name. She wasn't the one he was working the closest with at the time, so he hadn't paid her much attention. And with a few minor differences, Tylers seemed to all look alike. "Sorry about that."

She had tripped over him, but he didn't point that out. Part of his image was his charm with the ladies, *all* of the ladies.

Snapping at one who apparently couldn't see where she was going wasn't something he wanted winding up in the papers. He wrapped his hands around her small waist and helped her right herself. She just blinked at him, a reaction he'd caused in women before. Hunter smiled his most charming smile.

"I'm sorry, Mr.—I'm afraid I don't remember your name. You're the guy that's been working with Pan, right?"

Hunter knew he gawked at the woman. But the expression on her face told him she was serious. This woman didn't know who he was. Why? How was that even possible?

He didn't want to sound egotistical or arrogant, but he was a damned household name now. "Yes. I am Hunter Clark, the star of this little production. Which Tyler are you?"

"I'm Nikki. Pan's cousin."

"And what is it exactly you're doing for Bowles and this movie?"

"I'm one of Perci's court, like Pan. I'm actually playing their younger sister, even though I'm six months older. I'm not doing much. I got too much work of my own to do."

"And what is it that you do?" He still had his hands on her. Did she even realize that? He wasn't in too big of a hurry to take them away, actually. She wasn't quite as small as Pan but was still more than a head shorter than he was. Hunter wanted to lean closer. But he didn't. He knew how to control himself better than that.

He wasn't that hard up for a woman, after all. Not enough to mess with a woman like this one. She was the apple-pie, Mayberry type.

"I run the Stop In Time bookstore on Main." She wiggled, brushing against him. She was probably five-five and thin. He had a good ten inches on this woman. And probably at least that many years. She wasn't a librarian, but it was damned close.

Quiet, bookish, thick glasses, but pretty. Very, very pretty, when a man looked close enough.

Too bad he didn't have time to look closer. He needed to find his costar and check on her for himself.

33

FOR THE LONGEST TIME, JOHN THOUGHT THAT the redhead standing with Clark was Pandora. It was worse. If that woman turned, she'd probably be able to recognize him.

He and Nikki Tyler had been in the same class all through school. She'd been a quiet little blind freak most of it. Still, she was pretty enough behind her glasses. She did look a lot like that Pan one, though.

He entertained himself for a moment, imagining her naked. He didn't have much else to do, after all. She was built a bit better than her cousins, at least. Still skinny, but at least she had some curves, too. Yeah, he wouldn't mind getting Nikki Tyler naked someday.

The chest looked like she at least had a good handful for a man to grab onto. She hadn't always been that way. He remembered her being kind of flat and plain, especially when compared to her cousins. Apparently she'd grown into herself a bit.

He watched the great fancy actor talking to her, and smirked. Did Hunter Clark really find that blind little loser hot or something? Seriously not. Maybe the guy was just desperate. They were in Masterson County, after all.

John looked back toward the Masterson house. Pan had to be around somewhere.

And he was being paid damned good money to watch every move she and Levi Masterson made.

34

PAN DIDN'T HAVE A LOT OF FRIENDS IN THE town—the few women she considered friends all lived in the next county south. It was only since first Phoebe's marriage and then Pip's that they'd socialized in Masterson again.

They had good reason for it; her sister Pip had been attacked at the community center one night. She had narrowly missed being raped. The man who had attacked her had returned recently and nearly killed Pip, Perci, and Matt.

Pan would always be leery being in Masterson, but she loved spending time with the various cousins who populated the county.

And after a week recuperating from the accident, she'd been more than ready to grab a ride with Pip when Pip had headed in to meet up with Matt.

She needed to see people besides Levi and his brothers. Or Pip and Phoebe. She needed someone who could be objective.

And she needed to talk to her insurance company about her car. Soon.

But first—she needed someone to talk to. Her cousin Nikki had been working on the movie set several times over the last week—Rowland Bowles was using Nikki as a body double for Pan when needed since she wasn't that much bigger than Pan and had the same coloring. They'd do the shots of her face when they got a chance.

Her five female cousins were some of the best friends she could claim. And she liked it that way.

Tylers ran toward boys—there were twenty-two male cousins in her generation, and only she, her sisters, Maggie, and Nikki, Augie, Junie, and seventeen-year-old Em for the girls. A good deal of those male cousins were older. The eldest Tyler, Martin, was right around thirty-five or so.

Having so many male cousins around did have its drawbacks. For her, her sisters, and her female cousins.

Tylers could be a little overprotective, especially of the women.

Even more so after what had happened to Phoebe and Pip. And even Perci, she had been injured when Pip had. Perci had just gotten out of the cast three weeks ago.

None of the Tyler men were overjoyed at the prospect of the movie company that had flooded the town. It made it a little difficult for her to meet up with Nikki the way she had wanted. Nikki was actually closer to Pip and Perci's age, but since her two sisters rarely went into town by themselves, Pan was the one who saw Nikki, Maggie, and their younger cousins the most. If she had best friends, those two were it. Maggie had a job interview in the north corner of the county, so she wasn't able to meet them today. But Pan timed things so that she could hit Nikki's bookstore just as her cousin was heading out to lunch.

Nikki was one of the extras in the Rowland Bowles movie, but Pan did not think her quietest cousin was enjoying it. In fact, Maggie had pestered Nikki into doing it so Maggie didn't have to do it alone. Nikki planned to funnel all of the money she earned—she had a few lines in the movie—into her struggling business. A bookstore in the middle of Masterson—well, it was going to be a struggle for very long time. Most people ordered what they wanted off the internet these days. But Nikki's mother had opened the book store when Nikki had been just a small girl; she and her brothers had a sentimental attachment to the place. Nikki ran it, while her brothers ran their ranch just south of town.

Money was always tight. But money was always tight for the Tylers. Things had only marginally gotten better for her branch of the Tylers when her sisters had married the Mastersons, and her father and Levi had hatched this scheme around an experimental line of cattle that her father was pinning all of his hopes on.

A small brush of worry Pan did not want to feel hit her.

Levi and her father were investing so much hope into this experiment, she couldn't help but worry about them being disappointed.

She waited for Nikki to lock the doors to the bookstore. They had at least a five block walk ahead of them. And Pan was pretty achy from the still healing bruises.

In the rain.

Pan pulled the jacket she'd grabbed off the

hook by the back door of the Masterson home tighter around her shoulders.

She'd known when she slipped it on that it was *his*.

Somehow, she didn't think Levi would mind.

She didn't know why she'd grabbed his and not one of the others—Pip and Phoebe both had had jackets hanging right there that she could've borrowed easily. But she'd grabbed Levi's.

Freudian slip? No doubt. The man was driving her crazy. She didn't know what to do about him. Still, his coat was warm and smelled just like him. It made her feel safe; for some reason, she needed that today. Joel waited outside the diner, and Pan stopped for a moment to speak with her brother-in-law. Joel was the one who had actually changed their world. He had certainly changed Phoebe's—but only for good. Joel and Matt were the best brothers-in-law she could have, and she knew it.

It was just their brother she couldn't stop thinking about.

Leave it to Levi to completely confuse her; she'd been thinking about nothing for two days. He'd left with her father to go to Texas again. He hadn't wanted to leave her. Pan had seen that in his eyes when he told her goodbye just that morning. He hadn't known when he would be back, either.

Pan missed him. Seriously missed him more than she ever thought possible. It was pathetic. What did that say about her? She was not going to fall for Levi Masterson. She wasn't about to just fall in line—it wasn't going to happen.

She and Nikki headed inside the diner. Joel was waiting for someone, but he'd made a point of checking on her when she walked by. Her sister's husband seemed to think he had to assume the responsibility for her and her siblings. She liked Joel, but Pan needed to make her own way. Just to see if she could. She turned and followed her cousin inside the diner. It was time to put Levi away for now. At least until she figured out exactly how she felt.

35

LEVI WAS EXHAUSTED, BUT HE WAS GLAD TO BE back. And not just because it was good to be home. Levi just didn't trust that Pandora was behaving herself. He'd wanted to get someone in to help her with the house for a few days while she continued to heal; she hadn't exactly like that idea. And she had told him so. Fiercely independent, those Tyler women. Even little Pip would prove stubborn when she didn't agree with something her husband said.

He never would've expected it from just looking at the four sisters. They looked so quiet and docile, those four. Until a man stepped close enough to realize they each had a very distinctive bite. He loved Pan exactly the way she was. And Levi suspected he deserved the nips she gave him.

He barely made it back for his two o'clock meeting at the diner with Viv Preston's father. Vince Preston was dying—things needed to be settled between them. Vince had seen the writing on the wall before he'd reached out to Levi and Matt about them buying half his place.

Levi had wanted the neighboring spread for a long while. Vince wanted to leave his daughter a legacy, and Levi understood that. But working with Viv Preston was more than he wanted to contemplate. But...the Preston place was more than just strategic. It was a damned fine investment.

That that daughter seemed to think her father was trading the ranch to Levi for her was something he hadn't quite expected. He should have, though; the woman had hinted several times through the years that she wouldn't mind getting to know Levi better. But she'd always rather turned his stomach with her nasty attitude toward others. He supposed she was beautiful enough, but there was something about the way she looked at other people that had always made him leery.

Levi scooted his chair farther away from hers

and turned back to her father. They had some serious negotiating to do.

Levi looked up as a pair of strawberry blondes
walked into the diner.

It was official. He had Tyler radar, and he
knew it.

Every time he saw a redhead, he had to check
to see if it was one of them.

What was she doing in town already? How
had she gotten there? The only logical explanation
was that she'd borrowed one of his ranch trucks or
ridden in with one of her sisters.

He didn't have a problem with that, of course.
What he had a problem with was her doing too
much too soon after what had happened. Levi
looked at his dining companions quickly. He
wished them anywhere but there, at the moment.
What he wanted to do was cross the diner, grabbed
the lapels of his denim jacket, and lift the woman
wrapped in it right up off her feet and kiss her.
Make it clear to everyone everywhere that he was
hers. And she was his. But he couldn't do that.

He had to be responsible and spend his time
building his empire. Levi hoped to have kids to one
day inherit that empire, after all. Little blue-eyed
stubborn redheaded girls—just like their mother.

36

"So," Nikki started as they took a seat at the small booth by the window. "He's looking at you again. Even I can see that."

"He's always looking at me. I'm starting to get used to." She hadn't told her sisters anything regarding her relationship with Levi. Not that she really *had* a relationship with Levi, of course. She sighed and stared out the window for a moment; that was a lie, and she knew it.

There was something going on between her and Levi, and it was time she admitted it. Why couldn't this be easy? Why couldn't she sit down, make a plan, and know exactly what to do or what not to do where he was concerned?

Why did it have to be so darn confusing?

She and Nikki left their stuff in the booth seats, knowing that no one would bother it. Other than placing their order at the counter, she said nothing else at all. Not until they were almost ready to sit back down. She looked at her cousin, the one woman she had shared almost everything about regarding that man. "He's kissed me several times, Nik. And a few nights ago, after the wreck, he came into my room and held me. I..."

"That's...very romantic, Pan." Nikki blinked, her blue eyes the same shade and shape as Pan's behind her thick glasses. Nikki didn't see all that well—and would never be able to even drive a car —but she was still one of the most observant people Pan had ever known. "But that's part of the problem, isn't it? You don't trust *romantic*. You trust facts and figures, pen-and-paper plans. You've always been that way. He scares you. Because he's going by gut and emotion, wild attraction and feelings, right?"

37

Coming into town had been risky, but the thought of five hundred grand for taking out one of those damned Tyler women was too good to resist; he needed the money. Viv was for damned sure not going to give him what he needed otherwise.

At all.

That money was going to get him out of the United States, for sure.

But though John had hurt people before, he'd never killed one. He wasn't certain why Viv wanted the girl out of the way, either. Yes, that Masterson was all over her, but so what? Viv was hot enough—and rich enough—to grab any man in Masterson County she wanted.

Levi Masterson obviously wanted Pan Tyler. Any jackass could see that.

He had to admit she worked hard. Pan didn't seem to cause too much trouble. Unlike that asswipe brother of hers.

Pan definitely wasn't hard to look at, either. That Masterson asshole certainly thought the same thing. Guy followed her practically everywhere. John took a moment to look around, pulling his hat down farther over his face. He ran his hand over the now reddish-brown beard covering his face. It was a lot different than his natural blond. Between the hat, the beard, and the nondescript clothing, he looked just like any other Amish man out for the day. There weren't a lot of Amish in Wyoming yet, but there were a few. Enough so that no one in the town was looking too closely at him.

He followed Pan right into town. She hooked up with that pretty little bookstore cousin of hers. John swiped at his nose again as he watched her for a bit. Nikki was a pretty one, now. In spite of the thick glasses. John vaguely remembered asking her out once, but she'd blinked up at him and quietly told him that she wasn't allowed to date. That had been five or six years ago, when they were in high school, and he'd most likely been drunk at the time.

He'd probably dodged a bullet there. Her brothers were intense where she was concerned—like his brother had been with him. He missed his brother, and the loss of Tom could be laid right at the feet of those damned Tyler women.

John might as well do exactly what Viv wanted. Get Pan out of the way so Viv could have that Masterson. It would be simple to do.

Might as well get it done. No Tyler bitch was worth passing up half a million dollars in cold, hard cash.

He waited, and watched the diner. He grew angrier and angrier that he couldn't just walk inside and order up a barbecue sandwich and home fries like he wanted. Because of Tylers and Mastersons. Though to be honest, it was really Pan and her sisters. And that brother of theirs.

Phoenix had started it all when he'd killed Tom's wife in that wreck. John would never forget how that had hurt his brother.

Tylers had done it. Caused all of this.

When he saw the two redheads at the front table, he smiled at his good luck. They had made it so easy for him.

John lifted the rifle and sighted his target. And pulled the trigger.

They had just made things far too easy.

38

PAN SIGHED, AS WHAT HER COUSIN HAD SAID rang true. It was. That was the whole entire problem. "You'd make a killing if you ever got your psych degree, Nik." Her cousin was absolutely right. Levi terrified her in so many ways. "He scares me; you're right about that. I don't know what to do about it."

She turned her head and looked at him. She'd known he was in there the moment she'd walked in behind Nikki. Just known.

Levi was looking at her, too. Pan could always feel his eyes on her and had from the very beginning. He might have said that he'd first developed feelings for her that day they'd almost lost Phoebe and Joel, but he'd looked at her before then. And she'd known it. It was time she stopped lying. To both him and herself. She'd never been as attracted to a man before as she was to Levi Daniel Masterson. "I have no idea what to do about it."

Nikki leaned closer. "Have you ever thought about just—"

The window eighteen inches from where they sat shattered around them. Something hot and fiery shot across Pan's arm, knocking her down into the hard booth seat. It was then she saw all the blood.

39

People screamed. Yelled for others to get down. He'd recognized the sound of gunfire the instant it had broken out. All he could think about was Pan. Getting to her. The three dozen people in the diner were either hunkered on the ground or racing toward the rear of the restaurant.

Not him.

Levi fought the crowd to get to the two women who had been the closest to the window. He reached the table and grabbed the first strawberry blonde he could. Pan's pretty cousin Nikki. She was crying and had lost her glasses somewhere. Without them, he suspected she was completely blind.

Someone's hands were there to take her from him. He looked up into Rowland Bowles's worried face. "Take her, quickly. I don't know how badly she's hurt, and she can't see to get herself out of here."

"I know. I've got her."

Bowles took her gently, tucking her against his chest.

Levi turned back. Pan and Nikki hadn't panicked, at least. They'd been small enough to huddle together underneath the tabletop instead of exposing themselves to more gunfire by running.

But they had been directly next to the glass, and there was blood. A lot of it.

Her cousin had been covered with it, and so was Pan.

Levi fell to his knees beside her. "Pandora Claire, honey, look at me. Were you hit?"

Tyler blue eyes blinked up at him. He'd never forget the terror in those eyes—or the relief when she recognized him.

"Levi, I..." She blinked and pulled in a deep breath. And then, right before his eyes, she pulled herself together. His girl wasn't a wimp; he'd give her that. "The bullet went through my arm, and

I'm bleeding. The glass...I think your coat stopped most of it. It's my arm that got the worst of it. I think Nikki was hit. I need to check on her. Where is she?"

Never had he been prouder of her than in that moment. Pan could hold herself together, of that he had no doubt.

It was one of the things that had first made him fall in love with her that day. This girl was stronger than she looked, and he adored her for it.

"Bowles has her. She's getting taking care of."

"Someone will need to call her brothers. Let them know."

"Honey, I think the entire town knows by now. Joel's after the shooter, I'm sure. He'll catch him and make him pay. I promise." Levi helped her pull his denim jacket from her shoulders. Glass fell to the floor. Her upper right arm was bloody, but she was moving it freely. He grabbed the napkin dispenser from the floor where it had been kicked in the chaos. He pulled several of the brown papers free and pressed them against the wound in her arm. "Come on, honey. Let's get you over to Perci and Nate. Let them patch you back together again, ok?"

She shocked the hell out of him when she threw herself against his chest and just clung to him for a very long moment.

Levi scooped her up and carried her out into the street toward the approaching sirens.

40

Viv hadn't been able to run away. Not with her father and his damned wheelchair blocking her path. She wouldn't have been able to leave him, even if she could. How could she? He would have been completely helpless.

And it had been over almost before it had truly begun. Viv was still shaking. Her father had been pushed out of the path of everyone, thank goodness. She'd thought it had been Levi, and that didn't surprise her. He was quick like that.

She looked around for him. It took her a moment to find him, even though the diner was small. So many people were in the way. Like always.

Levi was pulling women from beneath the front table. Bloody women.

Tylers.

She fought a smile. She hadn't missed when that damned Pandora had walked in.

"Quit it! He's not interested in you," her father said harshly from near her elbow. "He wants *that* girl there, and he's the kind of man who goes after what he wants."

"He wants your ranch. I can give it to him." She bit back the sharp words and the anger. Viv loved her father; she truly did. But in his last days he'd lost whatever filters he possessed. And he was making it clear how much she had disappointed him yet again. All he'd wanted her to do was find a damned husband to help her run the ranch her father had worked his entire life.

Because he didn't trust she could do it. Hell, she didn't want to do it. She wanted the money from it, and that was it. If she could just get Levi...

But no. He wanted that girl.

For now.

41

THE PREPAID CELL RANG. ONLY ONE PERSON had that number, and he answered it quickly.

"Hi, Viv. Where's my money?" John paced back and forth in the old cabin while he waited for the answer. She'd ignored his texts for the last hour.

He was conflicted—riding a high knowing he had taken a life, and terrified out of his mind.

Those Mastersons and Tylers would be looking for the killer.

And they were enough to terrify anyone.

"You're not getting it, you idiot."

"What do you mean?" John stopped pacing.

"You hit the wrong Tyler. It was Nikki, you

asshole. Pan is just fine. All wrapped up in Levi's arms."

He winced. He'd had nothing against Nikki Tyler. Far from it. Still...

"I *need* that money. And whatever else you got for me."

"Screw you. I'm not paying for something I didn't get, and you can get your high from someone else."

It was the fear of losing his supplier that terrified John the most, and he knew it. No one else anywhere near there could give him what he needed—not like Viv could. Combine that with the loss of five hundred grand. Anger boiled inside.

John would make her pay.

Just like his brother Tom had wanted to make the Tylers pay for ruining his life. "Then I'm not keeping quiet about what you tried to pay me to do. What do you think Nikki Tyler's brothers will think if they learn you told me to do it? You'd better hope the sheriff doesn't find me soon, Viv. I'll never forget this."

John slammed the phone to the ground and stomped it beneath his boot. Damn her. He should have known Viv was jerking his chain.

She'd pay. He'd make sure of it. Viv was going to get exactly what she deserved.

It would serve her right if he got Pan Tyler away from Levi Masterson, all right. Give Viv exactly what she wanted—and let every Tyler and Masterson know exactly why he had done what he had done.

See Viv get with Levi Masterson, then!

42

"WELL, WHY THE HELL HASN'T SOMEONE stopped him?" Levi knew he was being unreasonable, but as he paced the waiting room waiting for Pan to be sewn back together again, he couldn't stop himself. Joel had stopped by the hospital to see how she and her cousin Nikki were doing. Levi had finally left Pan's side, but only because Nate and Joel had ganged up on him. She was with his brother Nate and her sister, after all. And someone needed to speak with Joel.

"I have men on it, Levi, but these things take time. You think I like this?"

"Hell no, I know you don't like it, but it's fact. Someone could have been killed today. And everyone's talking about how they saw John Rutherford out there! How am I supposed to just stand around and do nothing? Just what would you be doing if it was Phoebe?"

"Exactly what I am doing. Or did you forget that Phoebe could be a target of this bastard, too?"

"Or you could. All of us could. We need to find him, and we need to stop him now." Before he hurt her again. Levi fought back the instinct urging him to get his ass right back next to her.

To circle and protect. The way he was supposed to.

"What's Nate saying? How is she doing?"

"Stitches, and a damn scar. That's it. She got lucky. But the bullet went through her and lodged in her cousin's collarbone. They've got Nikki back in surgery now." Nikki, who hadn't done a damned thing to the Rutherfords in her entire life. Any more than Pan had. Or Phoebe or Pip or Perci. Levi looked at his brother. "Get men out there to find him, because you and I both know it's only a matter of time before the rest of those Tylers start hunting. Nikki's brothers are going to be pissed. And start hunting themselves."

Joel winced. Both men knew Levi was right. Nikki Tyler had three older brothers and that whole gaggle of cousins. Men who wouldn't be content to just sit back and do nothing.

"Just don't do anything stupid, Levi. Focus on keeping Pan safe, and that's it. Let my office focus on finding John Rutherford."

"You'd better find them fast, Joel, before I saddle up right next to those Tylers and hunt for him myself. That's my girl in there, and I'm not going to risk her ever again."

43

PAN SAT ON THE HOSPITAL BED AND LISTENED to what he had to say. She'd rarely seen Levi angry like that, but it was hard to miss the fury. For her.

Perci leaned closer as she applied the bandage to the wound on Pan's arm. "That guy's got it bad for you, Pan. And I don't think he's joking around. What are you going to do about him?"

She didn't have a clue.

Her sister finished with her arm, and Nate gave her a shot of antibiotics and a painkiller. The painkiller left her head a little woozy, but she was determined to leave the hospital on her own two feet.

Levi was waiting for her, like she'd known he

would be. In the diner, in that nanosecond after she realized what was happening, her first thought had been for him. Of whether he was ok, or hurt, or even dead.

Her second thought had been that he was coming for her. She had just known that Levi was coming for her. And he had. He had been there in the very instant she looked up. Like he always was. She'd counted on that.

That mattered.

What she was going to do about it, she didn't know. Maybe

It was time she revised her plans a little? Maybe it was time she just made a choice then stuck with it?

Maybe it was time. She didn't have to work for Levi any longer. She could go back home, help her father and Perci with the kids.

It would definitely work. It might make money tight, but she could find something online to do. There wasn't anything holding her back, if she wanted to leave. Just him.

But...it was time for truth. Pan didn't *want* to leave *him*. He looked at her when she walked closer, and he stepped away from his older brother. He and Joel really did look a lot alike.

But there was something about Levi that just made him stand out for her. Wasn't it time she acknowledged that? Wasn't it time she just stopped hiding behind her plans, and being so afraid? She knew why she had become so obsessed with planning out her future over the last two years. Since they'd lost their mother. It was all about control; she hadn't been able to control what had happened two years ago, any of it. But she controlled her plans now.

Although...it almost seemed like those plans were starting to control her. She didn't know how much longer she could live like that.

But she would not find her answer in anyone else other than herself. That was just the way it was going to have to be.

Pan held her hand out to him; knowing he would meet her halfway. He reached for her instinctively, just like she had known that he would.

44

SHE WAS QUIET; LEVI DIDN'T FORCE HER TO
say anything. He wanted to ask her how she felt,
how she was, if he could do anything to make her
feel better, but he didn't. A wise man knew when
it was best to just wait. Adrenaline had crashed for
both of them, no doubt. He'd probably have more
nightmares, this time of finding her bloodied and
dead in the midst of the diner. He knew it. He
loved this woman. Every day just made that more
and more clear to him. Every time he had almost
lost her pounded that into his head and heart completely.

He damned well loved this woman. It wasn't
about sex or attraction or Tylers and Mastersons. It

was about him and her and how much he loved her. Period. The depth of that love had finally hit him today when he'd seen all that red.

He pulled the truck into the drive and parked in front of the house. Pan had dozed off on the drive. No doubt Nate had given her something to make her sleepy. Levi headed around the front of the truck and pulled her door open quietly. It was easy to scoop her out and hold her close for just a minute. He stood there in his front yard, staring down at her for the longest time.

Until someone touched him on the shoulder; a soft brush that startled him. He turned slightly, his arms tightening around the woman who meant the world to him.

Phoebe stood there, a look of compassion and understanding in the blue eyes so much like Pan's. Other than the hair color, Phoebe resembled Pan the most of the other sisters. Same sweet, round little face, same big blue eyes, same killer expression when they smiled. He blinked. Sometimes it was hard to look at her and Joel when they were together.

His brothers Joel and Matt were the luckiest guys in the world. He knew that. And so did they.

His hold tightened even more. He could've

lost her today. Just what that meant sent him shaking.

"Get her inside, I've got the guest bed ready. We'll let her sleep tonight; the morning is soon enough for questions—for both of you."

He looked at the sky. It was nowhere near time for him to hit the hay. There was work to be done. There always was. "I need to head to the barn, check on the bulls. Swing by the calves. Their mamas."

Phoebe nodded, as she held open the front door for him to carry her sister in. "I've already started dinner; make sure you're in time to eat. I'll watch over her for you, I promise." There was something in her tone that told him she did understand. And that she approved. That it was just a given that he loved her sister. Because it was right.

45

WHEN SHE WOKE, THERE WAS A HANDSOME man sitting in the chair next to her bed, snoring. He'd changed into his customary sleep clothes—those gray shorts again—and nothing else. She half suspected that if he didn't live with a bunch of people, the man would sleep in the nude. A small smile hit her lips at that. Especially as she studied his body closely. She had brothers; she knew what men looked like—well, she knew what teenage boys looked like. She had all those cousins; it's not like she was naïve. She may have only kissed one, but she knew what men looked like.

Levi was a fine example of the masculine shape—of that, she had no doubt. His arms were strong, his chest and abs were well defined, and the thinnest line of dark hair ran down to disappear beneath his waistline. Her fingers tingled; she half wished she had the right to touch.

She'd seen Pip and Phoebe touch their husbands before, casually, easily—even for Pip, who was extremely shy—and at that exact moment, she envied them the right they had to touch the men they cared about.

She cared about Levi; that, she would never deny from this moment on. When she had realized that he was in there as well, that he could have been dead just yards away from her, something in her had shifted. Changed.

Make her see things a little bit more clearly.

Levi's eyes opened, and then he was looking right at her. "Honey, how are you feeling?"

"Like someone shot me." She didn't want to talk about her arm. She wanted to feel him hold her. Pan took a deep breath then held her hand out. To him. "Levi...will you hold me for a while?"

She didn't have to ask twice.

46

LEVI WANTED NOTHING MORE THAN TO HOLD her, hold her as tight as he possibly could. This was his world right there. And he had almost lost her.

Josh Tyler had positively identified John Rutherford as the man who had shot out the Masterson diner window. Pan and Nikki had been the most injured, but four other people had been hurt in the mad panic that had happened immediately after.

Pan and Nikki could have died. No one had realized it at the time, but the bullet that had lodged in Nikki's shoulder had just nicked an artery. The girl could have bled to death. Would have, if Bowles hadn't carried her to the nearby ambulance himself. It had been close.

It could have been Pan.

That's all he could think about. "Honey, I...I should go back to my own room, before I do something you're not ready for."

"Shouldn't it be my job to decide what I am ready for— when I am ready for it?" Her tone was even, direct. As was her gaze. Pan wiggled her thin little fingers at him. Luring him. "Come here. I really need you to hold me, remind me that we are both ok. Together."

Her fingers trembled and that told him the truth—Pan was serious. And still frightened. Of him? Levi's gut tightened. That was the last thing he wanted.

"Baby, are you afraid of me?"

She shook her head. "No...not of you."

"Of?"

"This. You, me. A bed. What could happen next. What I want to happen next." Her fingers wrapped around his, and she pulled lightly.

Levi went, his heart suddenly pounding at what she was implying. But...he didn't want his girl rushing into anything she wasn't ready for because of what had happened in that diner. He didn't want her feeling pushed at all. "Honey, what are you asking? I know this isn't a part of your plan."

"No. It wasn't. But...I think it's time my plan changed. I want...to plan with you."

He needed no more encouragement than that.

Levi wrapped his arms around her and showed her just exactly how much she meant to him.

47

When they were finished, she redressed—this time in his shirt—and cuddled close to his chest.

Exactly where she belonged.

She smiled shyly at him, red tinting her cheeks. He'd never seen a woman sweeter than his. "Honey...you are beautiful...so what's on your schedule for today?" He wanted her where he could see her until John Rutherford was found. Period. To do that, he'd have to know what she was doing at all times.

"Hunter and I have a scene together today; it's the one where I tell him goodbye."

"My favorite scene." He was teasing her, of

course. Clark hadn't been too bad. He'd flirted and made his interest known, but he hadn't pushed. In the movie, Pan's character had a mild romance with Clark's character, and then she returned to her fairy ways. There was nothing more heated than a kiss between them. It was a sweet story.

"It's the last one we have together, until edits."

"I want to know where you're going to be at today."

She rolled her eyes and put one fist on her hip. "You're not going to turn all caveman like Joel and Matt, are you? Getting underfoot all day when I have things to do?"

Levi reached out and hooked his arm around her waist. He brought her tumbling down on him —gently. She wasn't anywhere near fully healed yet. "Probably. You've seen my brothers. Once we Mastersons finally get our girls, we do what it takes to keep them. We can't have some man like Hunter Louis Clark coming in and stealing our girls, now can we?"

"You're a big doofus, Levi. If I wanted to be with a man like Hunter, I could be. But for some strange reason, I'm with you."

He grinned. "Say it again."

"Say what?"

"Say that you, Pandora Claire, are here with me. Because I'm the best Masterson of the lot, and you love me—just the way I am."

PAN ALMOST SAID IT; ALMOST DID EXACTLY what he wanted. But when she looked at the grin on his face, she held back. Just because. And to be honest, maybe she wasn't quite ready to say *I love you* just yet.

She thought she loved him. Otherwise, she would not have gone to bed with him. She just wasn't sure what was supposed to happen next. Other than hoping she had a minute or two with Pip just to help her figure things out a little bit. Pip was really good at helping people figure out what they were thinking.

"One day, Levi, your ego is going to get the best of you."

"Probably, but not today. Seriously, though, I am going to stick close to you today. Just in case. Make sure Clark isn't poaching my territory. In the meantime, I think we have a few minutes, and I really want to snuggle."

Pan let him do just that.

48

JOHN KNEW WHAT HE WAS GOING TO DO. IT WAS just a matter of waiting for the right moment. He'd have to get her away from Masterson for one thing.

It shouldn't be too hard to do.

Masterson loved those damned bulls of his, after all. He did the same thing to a bull in a pasture clear across the property from where they were making that stupid-ass movie.

And then he waited.

Just like he had expected, one of the hands went running for Masterson ten minutes before nightfall.

It was almost too easy. He watched Masterson

give Pan a clear set of instructions; she didn't like it, but she eventually nodded.

And then Masterson was heading exactly where John wanted him.

All that was left for him to do was get her away from that damned Hunter Clark.

49

Viv knew she'd been stupid. She never should have promised John Rutherford half a million dollars to kill Pan. It had been spur of the moment and she had known it was going to come back to haunt her.

He was a damned idiot—Joel Masterson would catch up with him eventually. And when Joel did, she had no doubt John was going to spill his entire damn guts.

The biggest part of her wanted to pack up what she valued and run. Run as far away as she could.

But that would leave her father alone.

Viv didn't know if she could do that.

She spent hours debating just how to make that work. Her father didn't have much time; everyone knew that. So she'd have to make the story good.

Somehow.

50

HUNTER SMILED DOWN AT PAN AS LEVI Masterson took off with one of his ranch hands, enchanted by the little smile that kept playing over her pink lips when she thought no one was watching.

Something had happened to the girl, something good.

He'd heard about the diner shooting just yesterday, but he didn't know any details—other than that one of the Tyler sisters had been involved. From the fresh bandage on her arm, he suspected he knew which one. She looked fine to him. Beautiful. With that just loved glow some women got when they were happy. In love.

Hunter suspected Levi Masterson had some-thing to do with it.

Sweet. If he was the type to get a kick out of romantic shit. Which he wasn't. He felt a pang, though, of slight envy. It had been a long time since he'd been with a sweet woman like this one in front of him. Since he'd had someone to even care enough about him to watch him work from the sidelines, like Masterson had for most of the day. And the guy hadn't wanted to leave her this time, either.

Masterson had barely taken his eyes off her in the last several hours.

"How are you feeling today?" he asked, when they had a few moments between their final scene and Bowles letting them all go for the day. "The diner?"

"Yes. I was there, but I was just nicked. My cousin Nikki is the one who was hurt the worst."

"Nikki, the..." Hunter's chest seized for a quick moment when he put it together. He hadn't been looking for the woman who had trod all over his ego today, but now that Pan mentioned her...

"The one with the thick glasses?"

The thick glasses and the sweet face, complete with girlish freckles over her nose. The one who ran a little used bookstore, of all things. Who probably sewed doll clothes or made cookies in her spare time.

That one. He must have thought about her half a dozen times since she'd tripped over his feet that day.

And she had been hurt in a random shooting? Damn, it must have terrified her. It had him all those years ago when he'd...Hunter almost choked on the emotion suddenly hitting him. Why did he care so much about a clerk from little Masterson, Wyoming? She was nothing to him. "Is she going to be ok?"

Pan nodded, her face oddly pale beneath the studio makeup still caking her face. It didn't help that the flood lights were behind them or that it had started to rain lightly. "We think so. She has a broken collarbone, from where the bullet hit her, and it bounced off an artery. Rowland carried her to the ambulance himself. We almost lost her. But she'll be fine. Perci's checking on her nightly, too."

The mere idea of what she'd gone through sickened him. "Good. Do they have any idea who or why?"

"A man with a vendetta against my family and Levi's. Joel will find him. They think it's a guy who we tangled with several months ago. His brother died when he tried to kill my sisters. Joel's the best."

Of course, the sheriff was. Everyone in this town idolized the Mastersons. "He's Levi's brother?"

The cheeks went red again. "Yes."

"I see. And your brother-in-law, then."

"Of course."

"Don't you think it's a little weird? Your three sisters with his brothers, and you with him? I could help you add some variety, if you like?" He grinned, letting her know he wasn't entirely serious. Hunter was an actor, after all. And he wasn't about to let her know that most of his attention was on a Tyler girl that wasn't even there. That girl hadn't deserved to be shot like that. Not like...well, Hunter knew the pain that kind of violence could bring. Knew it intimately.

"Perci is not with Nate. And don't let her hear you say that. It's a good way to get fried—"

Something hard slammed into the back of Hunter's head, sending him careening into her. Hunter tried to catch himself, but he couldn't. His head struck the base of a floodlight, causing pain for the second time in three seconds. He lay there dazed and unable to do a damned thing as a man he'd never seen before dragged Pan away.

He struggled to his feet and started after them. His feet slipped in the mud, and he went crashing down one more time, his head striking the concrete next to him.

51

Pan fought, but the man was on her before she could even react. She recognized him, even with the stupid disguise he wore.

John Rutherford laughed as she fought him. Pan did everything she could to get breath enough to scream. But his hands were on her neck. She couldn't breathe.

She rammed her knee toward his stomach. Rutherford turned, deflecting her far too easily. His hand tightened on her neck, cutting her breath completely.

Pan fought to stay conscious, but couldn't...

52

"Poison," Matt said, shoving a sheet of paper at Levi. "Arsenic, to be exact. Extra-large doses."

"Who the hell would do that?"

"I can think of one person," Nate said from behind him. Levi turned to look at the brother behind him, taking quick note of the dark blue scrubs Nate wore. He only wore scrubs when it had been a rough one at the hospital. Levi didn't want to think about what it could have been. "Where's Joel? Any news about Rutherford?"

"Not that I've heard yet." Levi shoved back the anger. "but Joel's still out there."

"We need to call him, let him know about

this," Matt said, looking at the body of the bull who had been less than a year old. Levi would have to call Deane in the morning and let him know what the true cause of death was.

This was going to be a bigger problem than he could have anticipated.

But at the moment, Levi didn't care. He looked back toward the floodlights where the film crew was no doubt finishing up.

He needed to get back to Pan. Something just didn't feel right.

53

HUNTER OPENED HIS EYES AND FOUND himself lying on a couch inside the Masterson home. A blue-eyed strawberry blonde with thick glasses stared down at him, yet another Tyler female at her side. "Mr. Clark, how's your head?"

"Splitting." He ignored the pain for a moment and studied her quickly. She was staring at him like he was a bug, completely without the awe that a lot of women looked at him with. All he saw was concern. Maybe—it didn't seem like she was focused on him much at all. Her arm was in a sling, and she looked pale. Shouldn't she still be in the hospital? It had been only two days since the shooting, after all. "Hi. I heard you were shot. How are you feeling?"

"I'm ok. Perci and Maggie are making me stay here today, though. Can you tell us what happened? We came around the back of the house, and there you were. We had some of the ranch hands get you inside out of the rain. Director Bowles has been looking for you; we sent Patton to find him and let him know you were hurt."

"I thought you were resting at the hospital. That's what Pan—" He'd been speaking with Pan right before someone had struck him, hadn't he? "Where's Pan? She was right there with me when I was hit."

"We found you in the backyard. Like you'd tripped." Nikki blinked at him again, making him feel like that bug.

"Pan was with me. And someone hit me. I didn't trip over my damned feet out there like an idiot." As the ramifications sank in, he forced himself to stand. "I think a man was there. He dragged her off into the woods. We need to get people looking for her. Now."

"I'll get Levi," the cousin said. "Nik, you ok with him? Not hurting too much?"

"I'll be ok, Mag. Just find Pan. Hurry."

Hunter took another long look at her.

Her hair was down around her shoulders and soft looking. Poor thing looked ridiculously vulnerable. Some man needed to scoop her up and take care of her.

If his head wasn't killing him and he wasn't so worried about Pan, he would have wanted to touch. She looked so perfectly real. Nothing about her was Hollywood fake. Hunter had missed women like her. Far too much for him to think about.

"Come on." She stood abruptly the instant they were alone in the room. So abruptly Hunter almost didn't get out of her way in time. "We need to help find Pan."

54

When Levi made it back to the last place he'd seen Pan, there was chaos. Perci and her brother Patton were yelling. Yelling for Pan.

Levi changed course and ran toward Pan's sister. He grabbed Perci and yanked her toward him, probably harder than he should have. "Perci, where is she?"

"We don't know. We think John Rutherford dragged her off into the woods." Perci's fear was hard to miss. Levi forced himself not to rush heedlessly into the woods. The only thing behind his place was a damned hill and the Preston place.

Why would John Rutherford be headed there?

"We know this for sure?" Nate asked from be-hind Levi.

"Yes. Hunter was hit, but he saw enough to say what way the guy took my sister."

"Where is Clark?"

"He and Nikki and Maggie headed to the Pre-ston place. They're going to get the people over there to block off their side of the mountain. We have to hurry!" Perci took off toward the woods lining the back of the property, less than ten acres behind the house.

Levi was right behind her, Nate on his own heels.

55

JOHN WAS STARTING TO THINK WHAT HE'D done had been as stupid as it no doubt was.

Pan was unconscious, and he half thought he'd killed her. He didn't want to. There was no point in it, and he truly didn't have much of a beef with her. She hadn't even been in the car when Sadie had been killed. She hadn't been up there on the mountain that day when Joel Masterson had killed Tom, either.

No, all she had was the misfortune of being hot enough to catch the notice of the man Viv Preston had decided belonged to her. Why should Pan pay because of Viv?

Any more than John should pay for what Tom

had planned and done to the Tylers. It wasn't right.

She shifted, coming to. He struggled not to drop her. He wasn't anywhere near as big as his brother had been. Thankfully, she was a smaller woman. He twisted her, yelling at her to be still.

Pan didn't cooperate. She kicked at him and bit his neck hard enough to draw blood.

John dropped her. On the arm that had a bandage on it. She cried out. He scooped her up again when he heard people yelling.

They were coming for her, getting closer. He just hoped Levi Masterson was one of them.

56

What they were doing was insane, but Hunter didn't say a word as Maggie Tyler drove the ranch truck over the potted road back behind the Masterson ranch like a real bat out of hell. She beat any Los Angeles driver he had ever come across. She terrified him.

He tried to fight the ache in his head as they bounced and jolted, but it was getting harder and harder.

A soft hand brushed over his arm. "Are you ok, Mr. Clark?"

"Call me Hunter. And I'll be fine. We just need to find Pan." How in the hell was going to the ranch behind Levi Masterson's supposed to help them find who had taken Pan? Hunter didn't understand it.

She leaned closer, but the rapidly darkening sky around them made seeing her difficult. "My brother works there. On the Preston ranch. He'll get the other people to help us look. And Perci will get the rest of the Mastersons. We'll find her. I promise."

He only hoped they were right.

Another bump sent the woman next to him careening right into his chest. Hunter's head bumped into hers, sending stars straight to his brain.

"Go faster, Mag. We need to get there before Gil heads home. If he does, we won't know anyone on the Preston ranch who can help us."

Hunter bit back a curse as the woman pressed harder on the pedal.

57

Viv was just about to go into her father's room and tell him she was going to have to leave him for two days. She'd made up a story about her mother's sister being in an accident and needing help.

He hadn't spoken to her aunt in years; she hadn't worried he would try to confirm, at least.

She'd just felt so bad for even thinking to deceive him right now.

If Pan Tyler just hadn't ruined all her plans, she'd have Levi right now. And everything would be all right.

If Pan and John hadn't screwed everything up for her she would have had everything she wanted.

Damn them.

Just as she finished packing her suitcase, the front door of the ranch she'd despised her entire life burst open.

She almost didn't recognize the man standing there in the frame.

But the strawberry blonde with terrified blue eyes was so damned distinctive.

Viv fought a scream.

58

PAN KNEW THAT THERE WERE PEOPLE somewhere that could help her. Her cousin Gil, Nikki's oldest brother, was the ranch foreman. He would be around there somewhere. All she had to do was get away from John. Somehow.

He shoved her into the house. "There, Viv. I got her away from your precious Levi. Just like you wanted."

"What?" It was the first time Pan had done anything other than scream since he'd hurt Hunter and dragged her away.

"Didn't know that, did you? Viv here is the one who wanted you gone. So she could have your boyfriend." John grinned.

The expression chilled her to the core.

Pan didn't waste time trying to talk. The instant Vivian Preston started yelling at Rutherford, Pan turned toward the door and ran.

She never made it. His hands tangled in her hair, and he yanked her to the ground.

59

LEVI JUST KEPT GOING. THE WOODED HILL behind his place wasn't an overly big area. Maybe six hundred and fifty acres or so. Still, that was more than enough for a man to hide for a while, at least. If he was smart.

Which John Rutherford most likely wasn't. But he had Pan.

Levi refused to let his fear make him do something stupid. The Preston ranch butted right up against his property, and they split the hill almost evenly between them.

If they could get enough people to start searching, they'd eventually find her. Trap Rutherford in between them all.

He just hoped it would be before Rutherford hurt her again.

They kept going until they reached the top of the hill. Until he heard her cry out. Levi started running.

Levi kept going. Nate and Perci had gone to the western edge of the woods, hoping that between them and the Preston ranch they could box Rutherford in long enough to get Pan back. It was the only real plan they had.

He made it to the front porch of the Preston ranch seconds before his brother.

Just as he heard a woman cry out from somewhere inside.

He didn't stop to think, Levi hopped over the steps. Levi grabbed the doorknob and threw the door open.

Just as Pan fell to the floor, John Rutherford on top of her.

Levi didn't stop to think, to even give a damn that the other man had a butcher knife in his hand. All that mattered was Pan.

He dove at the other man and shoved Rutherford to the floor. He yelled at Viv to call the sheriff.

And told Pan to run.

60

PAN WOULDN'T LEAVE HIM TO FIGHT A MAN with a knife alone. That was just not going to happen. She couldn't leave Levi any more than she could have left anyone else that she loved.

When she'd realized John meant to kill her and Vivian Preston, she'd been terrified. But seeing Levi wrestling with the man frightened her far more.

She couldn't lose him. Not like this. Not ever. She couldn't lose someone she loved again. Especially him.

Pan ignored the pain in her arm as she popped the stitches Nate had sewn himself. It didn't matter.

All that mattered was Levi. Pan forced herself to her feet and dove at Rutherford.

They all went down.

61

VIV NEEDED TO RUN. LEVI AND JOHN WERE tearing up the kitchen. Levi shoved the smaller man, and John slammed into the glass hutch, sending shards everywhere. Neither man stopped.

Pan was reaching for John, a fierce look on her own face.

Levi yelled at Pan to get out, to go outside where she'd be safe.

Pan didn't listen.

And she was blocking Viv's path to the door.

Viv's father yelled out from his room at the back of the house. He wouldn't be able to get to them, not without help.

He was her only regret.

Viv grabbed her bag off the table and ran for the door.

62

Oh, no, she wasn't. Pan didn't stop to think, but there was a reason John Rutherford had dragged her here to Viv Preston's place. And she was going to find out just exactly what it was.

She stuck out her leg and sent the woman sprawling. Viv went down with a curse.

Viv struck out. Her nails dug into Pan's arm. Pan didn't let go. She'd grown up with a ton of siblings—she knew how to fight. Anyone who'd lived with Perci Tyler knew how to hold her own in a catfight. It had been a matter of survival during her childhood.

The other woman kicked out, but Pan avoided

the three-inch heels. Who wore heels at seven at night on a ranch? That was just stupid.

"You bitch! You should have died!" Viv yelled, biting toward Pan's arm. Pan barely avoided the woman's teeth. Perci had liked to bite as a kid, too. And Pip would always join in with Perci, leaving Pan squabbling with two sisters at once. Until Phoebe would come to her rescue.

"Why did you tell him to kill me?" Pan grabbed the older woman's hair and yanked as hard as she could. Pan was strong from years of actual hard work, and it made a difference, even though the other woman was bigger, older, and not recovering from a car wreck or bullet wound.

Viv Preston had been pampered her entire life. She didn't stand a chance against a woman fighting for the man she loved.

Pan pulled her to the floor.

And sat on her. Viv wasn't moving until Joel came to take her away. Period.

63

HUNTER HOPPED OUT OF THE TRUCK AS FAST as he could when it came to a stop. He was never riding in a vehicle with Maggie Tyler again. The woman terrified him. Her smaller cousin didn't even seem to notice that Hunter's hand had gripped the door handle like a damned lifeline.

No, Nikki had barely waited until he got out of the truck before she was hopping to the ground and rushing toward the house.

"Nikki, wait!" Maggie yelled.

Just as a tall man with dark-red hair came running out of the barn. "Nikki!"

"Hurry! John Rutherford dragged Pan into the woods behind Levi's house!" Nikki didn't even stop moving, just running toward the porch. How in the hell was she even moving after what had happened to her recently?

Hunter wasn't about to let her go into that house alone. They didn't have a clue what they were going to find. He heard at least one man inside screaming.

He was two steps ahead of her. He reached for her and yanked her into his arms. "No! *You* are not going in there!"

"Keep the girls out here, Clark!" The tall cowboy yelled as he hopped up the stairs. In the bright porch light, it was obvious he was a Tyler.

Hunter looked down at the woman in his arms. "You stay out here. I'm going in there to help. Do not come inside, no matter what. Do you understand me?"

"Just help them!"

Hunter nudged her toward her crazier cousin and ran up behind the cowboy.

64

Every joint in Pan's body hurt, but Vivian Preston wasn't going anywhere. Instead, she just twisted and fought and yelled a variety of curses that almost shocked her. Except...Pan's brother Phoenix knew a lot more curses than this woman. Much more creative ones, too. But Phoenix had always been creative.

Nothing could shock Pan at that moment.

Levi was securing John Rutherford with curtain cords of all things. She watched him, taking in each strong, sure movement he made. The other man hadn't hurt Levi, thank God.

Levi had just finished tying John up like a calf

when her cousin Gil and Hunter Clark came rushing in.

"Pan!" Gil pulled her off of Viv Preston and hugged her. Viv came up swinging.

Hunter Clark grabbed her and held her arms down. "I'm not sure what's going on here? Why were you sitting on this woman?"

"Because she paid John Rutherford to kill me. Five hundred thousand, but he hit Nikki instead."

"Shit, she did!" Gil said. "Viv's a real piece of work, but I don't believe that, Pandora."

"Oh, she did. Because she wanted Levi for herself." Pan would never understand it. Levi wasn't a damned possession for Viv Preston to just demand or own. "John said...she offered him half a million dollars to kill me. But he missed and hit Nikki instead. He confessed it all."

Viv chose that moment to spew more filth—directly at Pan. And John.

Gil stared at her in horror. "That true, Viv? You the reason my little sister was almost killed?"

"He was supposed to hit her! I needed her out of the way." Viv practically wailed it, just as Joel and Nate and Perci and Matt burst in.

Pan finally stopped shaking. Their family was there. It was over.

And now every bump and bruise John Rutherford had given her was starting to make itself known.

Perci grabbed her first, wrapping shaking arms around her. "You ok? Did he hurt you?"

"Yes. But I'm going to be fine." Her arm was on fire—not the one that had stitches either, though that one didn't feel all that great. She looked down at the blood soaking her clothes. Rowland Bowles was going to have a lot to say about the condition of her costume. Good thing the movie was almost finished.

"He had a kitchen knife, and I think I got in its way."

Maggie and Nikki came in and joined the crowd around the Prestons' large kitchen.

Mr. Preston was still yelling out from somewhere. Gil looked at Pan and touched her cheek gently. "I'm glad you're safe, kiddo. If I had known Viv was causing all this trouble, I would have had her daddy stop her. I'm going to go take care of the boss. Let him know what's happened. This is the last thing he needs right now."

"Thanks, Gil. I'm sorry Nikki got dragged into this with Rutherford."

"Hey, one Tyler, all Tylers. You know that."

Her cousin hugged her quickly, then nudged her toward her sister.

And Nate. He was already grabbing paper towels and supplies, helping himself to whatever he needed.

But Pan didn't care. All she cared about was the handsome cowboy staring at her.

The one who had ruined all of her plans.

The man she loved.

Pan stepped around Perci and leapt. Straight into the arms he opened just in time.

Levi caught her. Just like she had known he would.

EPILOGUE

IT TOOK THEM FOUR HOURS TO FIGURE everything out with the sheriff's office. John Rutherford was giving them everything they needed, and he'd even texted Viv Preston, confirming the amount he'd receive for killing Pan.

Levi would never forget the evil that had been in that woman's soul. She had been willing to kill to possess him. And he didn't understand the why.

Pan's cousin Gil had told him quietly that he'd overheard Mr. Preston pressuring the woman to find a husband capable of running the ranch after he was gone.

Apparently, she'd decided she wanted Levi to be that man.

And nothing was going to stand in her way.

Especially someone she viewed as beneath her.

Viv had taken the smart route and gone quiet when Joel started to question her. She'd demanded an attorney. Joel hadn't pushed.

But Viv wasn't going anywhere, and neither was John Rutherford.

He was the last threat hanging over their heads. Levi was glad it was finished.

He had plans to make.

He'd finally got his woman, after all. And nothing was going to ruin that.

Nate took care of the small knife slice in Pan's arm while Levi held her on his lap. Perci was trying to take care of him. He'd need stitches in his own lip.

She and Nate worked ridiculously well together, barely needing a word between them, as he sewed up Pan and Perci sewed up Levi. Technically, she wasn't supposed to do sutures, he thought. She might not have been licensed for it, but she took care of him anyway.

Nate didn't stop her.

Perci kissed him on the cheek, and whispered in his ear. "Thank you for keeping her safe."

Of course, he had.

Pandora Claire Tyler was his entire world.

Pan looked up at him when his arms tightened around her. He ignored his brother and her sister for a moment. "I love you, Pandora Claire. Always. If any woman gets to have me, it's always and forever going to be you."

She was quiet—hell, the entire kitchen went quiet—as she stared up at him. But she didn't pull away.

In fact, the fingers of her free hand—Nate wasn't finished stitching her arm yet—tightened on his shirt. "I love you, you goob. You've ruined every plan I've made. And I just don't care anymore. All I care about is you."

Levi leaned down and kissed her, carefully avoiding his newly earned stitches. He didn't care if Perci had to do it all over again.

He wanted to kiss the woman he'd love forever.

And he did.

Keep your family close, but your enemy closer.

Everyone expects her to fall for him.

Perci Tyler wasn't having any part of it.

Her sisters had fallen—hard—for his brothers. But

that didn't mean Perci was going to follow the same path with her irritating, arrogant, jerk of a boss, Dr. Nathaniel Masterson.

It just isn't going to happen. She and Nate despise one another—why change something if it works?

But when circumstances force them closer together than ever, all the fight between them changes— shifting into something Perci can't define. It terrifies her.

Now she has no idea what she's going to do with the devil in the center of her world.

He wants her—and has from the first moment they met...

Everyone knows it.

His brothers, her sisters—the entire town of Masterson, Wyoming. Nate certainly knows it.

Perci is the only one who doesn't know just exactly how he feels.

She's made him ache for her—from the very beginning. Now, it was long past time he gave in to the temptation she presents...

Before the threat stalking them both ends any chance they have at forever.

His son was dead. Gone.

A victim of his own stupidity and youth and baser urges. Clive understood that. He wasn't a stupid man, nor was he blind to the ways of the world. His boy Jay had never been the best sort, nor had he been the brightest.

Dog mean, some had said about his younger son. His *real* son. His blood.

Clint was just the bastard his wife, Paula, had foisted on him the day they'd wed. He'd given the boy his name out of duty and obligation. Because the father of that boy had been his own brother, who'd taken off into the hills when Paula had said she was pregnant. Women in Masterson,

Wyoming, were hard to come by. He'd taken the first woman he could stand talking to who knew her way around the bedroom.

He hadn't truly regretted it. Paula had been a riot to play with. Always up for an adventure in the sack, too.

Ovarian cancer had taken her out of the world, and his life, when the boy she'd given him had been all of sixteen months old.

He'd had the raising of Jay and his older step-son, Clint, ever since. Jay had made some missteps along the way, but Clive had never expected his boy to end up like *this*.

His boy hadn't deserved to suffer like he had there at the end. No human being did. Hell, not even a dog deserved this.

Jay had made mistakes, but his boy had died in pain. No amount of drugs could completely dull the pain of the burns that would never have healed. Or the pain of losing the girl Jay had wanted.

That it was his boy's fault for setting the fire mattered little.

Those damned Masterson boys should have gotten Jay out faster than they had. It would have been the right thing to do.

Why couldn't they have done the right thing to do?

Clive collapsed next to his son's hospital bed as the tears almost destroyed him.

Jay hadn't deserved to die this way. Not because of some damned girl. It just wasn't right. Jay had deserved better.

Nathaniel Masterson, head of the Masterson County Hospital, waited around the small ER until the woman he needed finally showed up. She'd been somewhere in the back of the small ward, helping with an MVA patient who'd needed her mother. The mother was currently in ICU with a very cautious prognosis.

It had been a longer night than he even wanted to think about. But everyone would live, barring any complications.

And he—*they*—still had a forty-minute drive to the ranches where they lived. He checked his watch. Nate had moved Persephone Tyler—his nemesis and thorn in side—to the later afternoon/early evening shift months ago. He'd had her on three p.m. to three a.m. but that had had to change.

It was just too dangerous for a woman to be out that late.

Even in Masterson County.

Recent events in the town that had nearly killed all three of his brothers—and all three of Perci's sisters—had made that abundantly clear to him.

Nate wanted Perci on the same shift he was on.

Easier for him to keep an eye on the little trouble magnet that way. Trouble just had a way of finding *her*.

She was the type of woman a smart man never turned his back on. That man had to keep his wits about him at all times.

Nate was stuck with her as a major part of his life; she was sister to all three of his sisters-in-law. He adored the three other Tyler women. There wasn't anything he wouldn't do for the women his brothers loved.

That meant Perci was *his* responsibility when at the hospital. More so than anyone else, though he took the safety of the rest of his staff seriously, as well.

But Persephone Tyler...Perci was *his* to watch over. He'd felt that way about her from the very beginning. Long before her sisters had captivated his brothers.

He'd known her and wanted her long before they had ever met her sisters.

Nate found himself wanting to watch her far more than a smart man should.

She dragged in, fatigue clear in her Tyler blue eyes. And limping. He'd heard the story—one of her patients tonight had had a massive seizure. The man was nearly as big as Nate; Perci had been knocked to the floor during the event. She'd done some damage to a not-quite healed fracture in her leg she'd suffered recently.

He'd told her a week ago she should have still been in the cast. But she'd insisted it come off.

She would never complain, especially to him. He called her name and motioned toward his office door, right off the main lobby.

Her shoulders slumped and a wariness hit her face, but she nodded. Nate studied her as she limped toward him, clutching the crutch that one of the orthopedic physicians had insisted she use for a day or two. The physician had had a tough time getting her to agree—but he'd eventually managed. Nate had commiserated with the man an hour ago.

Perci eyed Nate like he was about to bite.

She felt about him the same as he felt about her. They were two tigers caught in a cage, ready to defend their small space from the other. Nipping and snarling, biting and clawing.

Perci rubbed her face with one hand. She was paler than normal. The freckles on her cheeks stood out like paint spots. "What is it, *sir*?"

She always called him that when they were on the clock; it was another one of her little ways of poking at the bear. Perci loved to poke the bear.

Nate was the damned bear, and he knew it.

"Inside my office. We have some *family* business to discuss."

"We're not *family*, Dr. Masterson. Not you and I. You're the one Masterson I'm not going to claim. How many times do I have to tell you that?"

"Ha ha. We're *kissing* cousins. You might as well get used to it." He'd like to kiss her. Just to stop that little mouth from snipping at him all the time.

But if he ever started kissing her, he'd probably never want to stop.

"Just because my sisters went all loony over a

bunch of Masterson cowboys doesn't mean I'm as gullible. Trusting. Naive. Willing to be so stupid." Her smirk was weak. It had him mentally sighing. Why did she always have to *fight*? Especially him.

It seemed like they'd been fighting since the moment they'd met. She was tired and hurting, and still hissing like a half-wild kitten.

"You think your sisters made mistakes?" He knew she didn't; Perci was a strong supporter of her new brothers-in-law in everything. It was just Nate she didn't like.

His fault. He hadn't exactly gone out of his way to play nice with this woman. He'd done everything he possibly could to push her away.

"No. But only *three* of you brothers were good husband material. And they snatched them all up. Not everyone in a family can measure up." She shot him a sassy look, though the exhaustion in her face and in the way she held herself told him its own story. "I don't suppose you have a cousin somewhere for me? I met one or two at the weddings who would work."

He'd not wanted to admit it to anyone, but he'd been worried about her tonight.

It hadn't been all that long ago that she'd been injured by a burning beam when a monster had attacked his brother and her identical twin. Perci's actions had saved all of their lives—and she'd ended up with second-degree burns on her back and a few broken bones. She was still healing.

Still looked so...vulnerable. Nate hated when Perci was vulnerable.

Her family had had its share of troubles in the past year. That, no one could deny.

What he had to tell her would just wrap all that up. Tie the loose ends. Hopefully, the Tylers could move on after that.

Like Perci's three sisters Phoebe, Pip, and Pandora, all had.

Sparring with Perci just hadn't been the same since the night Jay Gunderson had burned down the Tylers' barn, with Perci, Pip, and Nate's brother Matt inside.

"Jay Gunderson is dead. Complications from an infection. I thought you deserved to know as soon as I learned."

Perci stared at him out of those eyes of hers that he still dreamt about. "I'm not exactly sure what I am supposed to say here."

"I know." The loss of life, any life, had always struck him hard. But in this instance, he just couldn't force himself to mourn the man who had tried to kill the woman in front of him. Who had tried to kill Matt. And Perci's twin, Pip, who had never hurt anything or anyone in her entire life. "But I wanted you to hear it from me."

She nodded. "Thank you. I'll tell Dad."

"I've already called Matt to let him and Pip know."

She nodded again. "Of course. Just what she needs. Reminding of Jay Gunderson. She's not feeling well today."

"You spoke with her?"

"No." It was a simple answer, but Nate didn't press. He knew how she operated. And damn it all, even though it belied all logic, Perci always seemed to know exactly how her identical twin was feeling. Especially since Pip had announced her pregnancy. "But I know."

"That's a little too woo-woo for me."

"Your powers of description are awe inspiring, Dr. Nate."

He snorted. "Grab your things, smart ass, and let's go. I promised Matt and Joel I'd drive you home tonight."

"Gee, thanks, Galahad."

But she followed along. Which told him her

exhaustion went deeper than her desire to avoid him at all costs.

She said very little as they drove. About twenty minutes into the drive, he looked over at her. She hadn't spoken in a while.

"You ok?"

"Just thinking. Tired. Dr. Paterson gave me something for the pain. It's getting to me."

"Admitting a weakness? You must be hurting worse than I thought?" All joking aside, he wanted to know.

She went silent and stayed that way until they got to his home. He hadn't intended to bring her there, but he had.

Perci hadn't said a word when he'd made the turn into the private access road that would lead to his place, instead of going past it on toward the Tyler ranch several miles beyond.

It wasn't until they were in his driveway and he'd rounded the front of the car that he realized she'd drifted off.

Nate made a quick decision. She didn't need to be putting weight on that foot. Not when she didn't have to.

He opened her door and leaned down.

Startled blue eyes met his. "Nate?"

"Yes."

"Why am I here?"

"I made an executive decision—as your physician."

"Dr. Paterson treated me tonight."

"He gladly turned your care over to me after you snipped at him tonight. So...I made a decision. You're sleeping here tonight. Where I can keep an eye on you."

"It's just a sprain, you dork."

"And it happened on my watch. You're stuck with me tonight. *Unless* you can get Pan or Levi to drive you home? It is rather late..."

She sighed, then turned her face against his neck. He half feared she'd bite him. "I can walk, Masterson. I'm not helpless."

"Can it. You're dead on your feet. And probably a bit wobbly. You should have two crutches, not one. The instant I put you down, you'll fall and break your neck. Sue the shit out of us."

"Right. Like I'd sue my three brothers-in-law—how would they support my future nieces and nephews?" She squirmed. "Put me down, you idiot."

"No." Nate knew he was being a contrary ass, but she'd acted like he was a serial killer out to carry her off. Besides, he was enjoying it. Perci smelled like all woman. The scent of hospital antiseptic and cleaner was still there, but he could make out her shampoo, too. And the unique scent that was all *her*. "It's raining, and you'll fall flat on your ass—or break that leg again."

He wasn't an idiot. His attraction to this woman was stronger than any he'd ever had for another woman.

Perci was the woman he would dream about at night for a long, long time.

Sometimes that attraction got the best of him, and he did something stupid like this.

He scooped her up and carried her over the steps and onto the front porch.

The door opened, and his brother Levi stepped out. "Caught you a pretty fish, too? *Finally*. I told my wife you were the slowest on the uptake."

Levi's words had deepened with satisfaction at the word *wife*. All of his brothers sounded just like that when they mentioned the women they loved. Matt and Pip were now fully ensconced on their ranch a mile or so past the entrance to this one that Nate currently shared with Levi. This one had been the family homestead for generations. Levi ran the ranch—all the properties, mostly—owned by the Mastersons, while Nate's brother Joel ran the county as sheriff, and Matt ran a successful vet practice and worked toward building his own horse ranch. Joel and his wife, Phoebe, lived a bit closer to the town now, having finished redoing the old homestead that had been Nate's grandparents' place. There was one smaller chunk of property with a three-story, four bedroom home on it. It was about five miles west of where he now lived. Levi owned two of those miles in between. Matt owned one, and Nate owned the rest.

One day, if Nate ever married, he'd take his own wife there. He was almost finished with the renovations now.

It was just a matter of another week or two.

He'd been thinking of moving there a lot lately. Hard not to do, when his house was constantly filled with his brothers and the women they loved. Redheaded, blue-eyed women everywhere he turned. Each and every one of them reminding him of the one in his arms.

Perci was always around now, too. Never far from her sisters. They traveled as a damned pack; that was for certain. Every time he blinked, she was there.

Tempting him to do something completely stupid. Like touch her. Kiss her.

Give her his entire soul.

"Can it, Levi. She's exhausted and took a hard knock tonight when a patient fell on her. Hurt her ankle and leg again. I just gave her a lift. She's had some pain meds and is extremely groggy."

"Sure, you did." Levi smirked at him, then looked at Perci more closely. "She looks more like a captive. That your intention? Carry your woman away? Let me guess, taking Persephone down to Hades? I was going to try it with Pandora if she didn't start cooperating, but I figured she'd emasculate me if I even tried. I *thought* Perci was the scariest sister, but I've learned. Pan has her beat hands down."

"He's lucky I don't have a scalpel."

Perci was just glad it was so dark her brother-in-law couldn't see the red on her cheeks. Levi was the type to snark at her for what his brother was doing. And what in the hell *was* Nate doing? "I can walk. He just likes to lord it over me that he's bigger and stronger and in charge—at the hospital. I *thought* he was driving me home."

"Aha. He captured you when you were least expecting it. I'm not going to ask what Hades is planning to do with you, Persephone, but I can imagine."

"Ha ha, Levi." She thought about squirming again. But the arms around her were far too strong for that to do much good. She would just keep her dignity and let this play out how it would. That was all she could do.

But, damn it, she did feel like a captive.

With Nate, it was best to just let him *think* he was winning. She'd just do that until he decided to let her down.

Sometimes it stunk, having him so much bigger than she was. Perci suspected Nate liked the size difference. Liked having her vulnerable and in his clutches.

Hell, that drug was making her a bit too dramatic tonight. She squirmed slightly, but the arms around her were hard and strong. She wasn't getting down until he chose to *put* her down. Period.

He smiled down at her, but there wasn't any humor in the expression.

More like a mountain lion about to pounce.

That was usually how she felt about the man. Like he was going to attack her at any moment.

Past history had told her she wasn't that far off the mark with him. Give him an opportunity, and he definitely would pounce.

"You can put me down, Masterson."

"Nope. It's a matter of principle, now."

"Excuse me?" The man didn't make a lick of sense. Except that he'd always enjoyed making her life as difficult as he possibly could. She squirmed again. His arms tightened.

Nate had really strong arms that she knew would never drop her, at least. There was that. The man was going to keep her safe—all while annoying the hell out of her.

"Inside. Then you can camp out in the guest room. If you really want, I'll drive you home in a bit. Your dad home tonight?"

She shook her head. Her dad had been splitting his time between his partner's ranch in Texas and theirs, lately.

"The boys?"

"No. Phoebe and Joel have them," Levi answered. "So our sweet little Perci would be left all alone over there."

"Exactly."

Her younger sister Pan snickered when he walked by her. She'd been the one to flick on the light. "Watch out, Perci. You're next."

"Bite me, Pandora. Just because the rest of you lost what brain cells you have the instant you saw a Masterson doesn't mean *I* will."

"*Sure,* you won't..."

ALSO BY CALLE J. BROOKES

ROMANTIC SUSPENSE

PAVAD: FBI ROMANTIC SUSPENSE

Beginning (Prequel 1)

Waiting (Prequel 2)

Watching

Wanting

Second Chances

Hunting

Running

Redeeming

Revealing

Stalking

Ghosting

Burning

Gathering

Falling

Hiding

Seeking

FINLEY CREEK SERIES

TRILOGY ONE (TEXAS STATE POLICE)

Her Best Friend's Keeper

Shelter from the Storm

The Price of Silence

TRILOGY TWO (FINLEY CREEK GENERAL)

If the Dark Wins

Wounds That Won't Heal

Hope for Finley Creek (bonus novella)

As the Night Ends

TRILOGY THREE (FINLEY CREEK DISASTER)

Before the Rain Breaks

Lost in the Wind

Walk Through the Fire

MASTERSON COUNTY NOVELLA SERIES

Seeking the Sheriff

Discovering the Doctor

Ruining the Rancher

Denying the Devil

SMALL-TOWN SHERIFFS

Holding the Truth

SUSPENSE/THRILLER

PAVAD: FBI CASE FILES

PAVAD: FBI Case Files #0001

"Knocked Out"

PAVAD: FBI Case Files #0002

"Knocked Down"

PAVAD: FBI Case Files #0003

"Knocked Around"

PAVAD: FBI Case Files #0004

"White Out"

PAVAD: FBI Case Files #0005

"Buried Secrets"

Calle has several free reads available at
www.CalleJBrookesReads.com

For my grandfather, the best man I have ever known.

You will be missed.

Oct. 2015

For my grandmother, who gave me the courage to try.
Without you and your love of romance, I never would
have made it this far.

Feb. 2016

For my papaw, whose children loved him deeply, and
will always miss him.

Oct. 2017

Calle J. Brookes enjoys crafting paranormal
romance and romantic suspense. She reads almost
every genre except horror. She spends most of her time
juggling family life and writing while reminding herself
that she can't spend all of her time in the worlds found
within books. CJ loves to be contacted by her readers
via email and at **www.CalleJBrookes.com**. When
not at home writing stories of adventure and wrangling

with two border collies and a beagle puppy, CJ is off in her RV somewhere exploring the beautiful world we live in, along with her husband of she can't remember how many years and their child.